***The twins were becoming very fond
of Mack very quickly.***

They didn't want to lose him, the way they'd lost
the father they had never known. They wanted their
mommy to tell them they could keep Uncle Mack
forever, and that yearning had to be nipped in the
bud. She didn't want her daughters' hearts broken
when Mack left Tucson.

And *your* heart, Heather? she asked herself. When
she'd hugged Mack to thank him for the beautiful
vase, she'd been struck by a sense of being where
she belonged, encircled in his strong, protective
arms. And she'd felt the raging, burning heat of
what she knew was desire, of a woman wanting
a man, wanting to make love with that man.

Stop it, she admonished herself. This was
ridiculous. She hardly knew Mack Marshall.
Desiring him, wanting him was terrible, frightening
and—

It had been many years since she'd been made to
feel special and pretty and feminine....

Dear Reader,

It's the little things that mean so much. In fact, more than once, "little things" have fueled Myrna Temte's Special Edition novels. One of her miniseries evolved from a newspaper article her mother sent her. The idea for her first novel was inspired by something she'd heard a DJ say on her favorite country-western radio station. And Myrna Temte's nineteenth book, *Handprints,* also evolved in an interesting way. A friend received a special Mother's Day present—a picture of her little girl with finger-painted handprints and a sweet poem entitled "Handprints." Once the story was relayed to Myrna, the seed for another romance novel was planted. And the rest, as they say, is history....

There are plenty of special somethings this month. Bestselling author Joan Elliott Pickart delivers *Single with Twins,* the story of a photojournalist who travels the world in search of adventure, only to discover that *family* makes his life complete. In Lisa Jackson's *The McCaffertys: Matt,* the rugged rancher hero feels that law enforcement is no place for a lady—but soon finds himself making a plea for passion....

Don't miss Laurie Paige's *When I See Your Face,* in which a fiercely independent officer is forced to rely on others when she's temporarily blinded in the line of duty. Find out if there will be a *Match Made in Wyoming* in Patricia McLinn's novel, when the hero and heroine find themselves snowbound on a Wyoming ranch! And *The Child She Always Wanted* by Jennifer Mikels tells the touching tale of a baby on the doorstep bringing two people together for a love too great for either to deny.

Asking authors where they get their ideas often proves an impossible question. However, many ideas come from little things that surround us. See what's around you. And if you have an idea for a Special Edition novel, I'd love to hear from you. Enjoy!

Best,
Karen Taylor Richman, Senior Editor

Please address questions and book requests to:
Silhouette Reader Service
U.S.: 3010 Walden Ave., P.O. Box 1325, Buffalo, NY 14269
Canadian: P.O. Box 609, Fort Erie, Ont. L2A 5X3

Single with Twins

JOAN ELLIOTT PICKART

SPECIAL EDITION™

Published by Silhouette Books

America's Publisher of Contemporary Romance

For Josh
who has learned how to smile

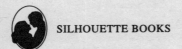 SILHOUETTE BOOKS

ISBN 0-373-24405-3

SINGLE WITH TWINS

Printed in U.S.A.

JOAN ELLIOTT PICKART

is the author of over eighty-five novels. When she isn't writing, she enjoys reading, gardening and attending craft shows on the town square with her young daughter, Autumn. Joan has three all-grown-up daughters and three fantastic grandchildren. Joan and Autumn live in a charming small town in the high pine country of Arizona.

SILHOUETTE MAKES YOU A STAR!

Feel like a star with Silhouette.
Look for the exciting details of our new contest
inside all of these fabulous Silhouette novels:

Prologue

The air was thick with smoke from the burning buildings and had an eerie orange cast. It even tasted strange, like dirt, charred wood...and fear.

Bullets thudded into the low, block wall with a maddening tempo as Mack Marshall crouched next to the old man and woman who were clinging to each other, trembling with fright.

"Hang on," Mack said. "The good guys know we're pinned down back here. They'll get us some cover fire and we'll make a run for it."

The couple stared at Mack with wide, terror-filled eyes. Their expressions told him they hadn't understood a word he'd said.

Damn, Mack thought, he'd really done it this time.

All the other photojournalists had pulled back. But him? Hell, no, not Mack Marshall. He had to get closer, to go for a few more pictures that no one else would get, to push his luck right to the edge. Luck, which was obviously running out very, very quickly.

He could die here. He could actually get shot full of holes and die in the dirt in this godforsaken place, his lifeblood seeping into the ground to be trampled by strangers' feet and forgotten, as though it had never been there. As though *he* had never existed.

Damn, he could die here...and no one would cry because he was dead.

Mack shook his head slightly in self-disgust at his depressing thoughts, but there was nowhere to escape from the chilling truth. Yeah, sure, he had friends scattered around the world who would feel badly that Mack Marshall had finally pushed his luck too far, once too often, and had bit the big one.

Mack was a helluva photojournalist, they'd say as they raised drinks in a final tribute to the reckless man who had never been without a camera around his neck and dynamic words to describe what he had seen.

Mack deserved all those awards he'd received over the years, they'd decide, filling their glasses again, but...by the same token...he sorta deserved his comeuppance too because he continually pushed his luck to the point of ridiculous and had finally paid the piper for the risks he'd taken.

Here's to Mack. Drink up, boys... The king is dead and which one of us will be the next king? Here's to

Mack...what was his last name again?...oh, yeah, Marshall. Mack Marshall... Did you notice there was no family at the memorial service for Mack?

No one.

There was nobody there who cried.

A bullet zinged through the air above Mack's head and he ducked even lower, cursing under his breath as he was pulled roughly from his dreary, mental ramblings.

The old couple gripped each other tighter, closing their eyes, their lips moving with whispered prayers.

"No," Mack said, shaking the man's shoulder. "Stay alert, be ready to run. Don't give up now. How are you going to see the terrific pictures I took of you two if you quit on me now?

"Never let it be said that Mack Marshall didn't take the extra step to get the perfect photograph, the one that puts him a cut above the herd. The picture that this time just might be the one that got him killed."

The old man and woman bobbed their heads in jerky motions, willing to hang on to the sound of Mack's deep voice, grasping at anything that hinted at hope.

Mack stiffened suddenly and narrowed his eyes.

"That's it. Hear it?" he said. "That gunfire is from the good guys. Yeah, I can see them up on that rise, and they're giving us cover. This is our last chance." He crept behind the couple and gave them a push. "Run. Now. Go!"

The elderly couple ran, hunched over, moving as

quickly as they could. Mack was right behind them, bending low, one hand flat on the old man's back to propel him forward.

They had to get to that building across the street, Mack's mind hammered. Go, go, go. Ten more feet. Five. Move, move, move. Almost there now...three feet left and they would be safe and—

A bullet slammed into Mack's left shoulder, the force of the impact causing him to fall onto his back in the dirt. White-hot pain rocketed through his entire body as a black curtain began to descend over him.

No! his mind yelled. He'd seen the friendly hands reach out and pull the old couple into the building. He had been one stride away from escaping the danger in the street.

And now he was going to die? Here? In the dirt? He was only thirty-seven years old, and he was going to die in a village in a remote part of a country that half the people in the world had never even heard of, or gave a damn about?

He was going to die alone, knowing that when the final words were spoken over him, no one would cry?

No-o-o!

Then everything went black.

Chapter One

Two months later

Heather Marshall leaned back in the chair in front of the computer and rotated her head, attempting to relax the tightened muscles in her neck. She gave up relief as a lost cause and directed her attention to the row of numbers on the monitor.

Nodding in satisfaction, she pressed the save button, then exited the program. A moment later she turned off the computer and sighed as blessed silence fell over the bedroom, the hum from the machine stilled after another day of work.

She got to her feet and glanced longingly at the

double bed that beckoned to her to crawl between the cool sheets.

"I'll be back," she said to the bed, pointing one finger in the air.

Leaving the cramped bedroom, she walked down the short hall to the living room, her destination the kitchen where she would pack the girls' lunches for school the next day. The brown bags would be waiting to be grabbed from the refrigerator as the twins prepared to make their usual last-second dash to catch the school bus.

When she was halfway across the living room, a quiet knock sounded at the front door, causing Heather to stop and glance at her watch.

It was nearly ten o'clock, she thought, frowning. Who on earth would be knocking at her door at this late hour? There must be an emergency with one of her friends in the neighborhood.

Heather hurried to the door, then hesitated as she gripped the doorknob.

Slow down and think, she told herself. Granted, the people in the dozen houses on her short block looked after one another, were like a family of sorts, but that didn't erase the fact that this section of Tucson was not the pride and joy of the chamber of commerce.

The small homes were old, the people who lived in them were low-income, struggling-to-get-by folks, just as she was. It was a high-crime area and only a dope would fling open the door at ten o'clock at night without knowing who was on the other side.

She went to the front window and peered through the drapes, clucking her tongue in disgust as she saw that the light had burned out—again—leaving her tiny front porch in total darkness. There was definitely something faulty in the wiring in that socket that caused the bulb to burn out within a few days of being replaced.

The knock was repeated.

Heather went to the door. "Who is it?"

"Mrs. Marshall?" a man's voice said. "Heather Marshall? I realize that it's late but I saw your lights on and...I was wondering if I might speak to you? It's really very important."

Heather narrowed her eyes and planted her hands on her hips.

"Are you selling something?" she said. "At ten o'clock at night? I'm not interested, thank you."

"No, no, I'm not a salesman," the man said. "Look, my name is Mack Marshall. I've been trying to locate you for weeks and now that I have I didn't want to wait until tomorrow to speak with you. Did you catch my last name? It's Marshall. We're related...kind of. I'll explain everything if you'll open the door."

Marshall? Heather thought, frowning. Mack *Marshall?* And he was claiming to be related to her? That was nuts. Her husband, Frank, hadn't had any relatives. No one. Like her, he'd been alone in the world, just one more thing he'd claimed meant they were to be together.

"You have the wrong Marshall," Heather said. "My husband has no family. Good night, Mr. Marshall. I hope you find who you're looking for."

"Wait," the man said. "Your husband's name was Frank. This is obviously as much of a surprise to you as it was to me, but I'm Frank's half brother. I didn't even know he existed until a few weeks ago. Then I discovered he died nearly seven years ago, but that he left a wife and children. I've been searching for you ever since. Please, Mrs. Marshall, won't you let me speak with you?"

Frank had a half brother named Mack? Heather thought incredulously. Was this some kind of scam? Oh, that was silly. What was this Mack Marshall person going to scam her out of? Her millions?

Mmm, she thought, pressing one fingertip to her chin. What to do? What to do? Mack Marshall had piqued her curiosity, that was for sure. It wasn't every day—well, night in this case—of the week that a long-lost relative popped up out of the woodwork.

Why hadn't Mack Marshall known until now that he'd had a half brother? And by the same token, why hadn't Frank been aware of Mack's existence?

Mmm. The safest thing to do would be to tell this Mack guy to come back in the morning, when she wouldn't feel as vulnerable as she did now when it was pitch dark outside.

Right, Heather thought dryly. That would result in a long night of tossing, turning and the piling up of unanswered questions regarding the mystery now standing on her porch.

"I give up," she said, then opened the door a crack to peer out.

Darn, she thought. That decisive action had accomplished nothing more than to give her a glimpse of a tall person barely silhouetted in the darkness.

"I've frightened you, haven't I?" The man said. "I'm very sorry, Mrs. Marshall. I've waited this long to talk to you so I'll come back in the morning, if that's all right. It certainly wasn't my intention to make you uneasy about letting me into your home. Is there a time tomorrow that would be good for you to speak with me?"

"Oh, for heaven's sake," Heather said, flinging open the door. "Come in. But, I swear, if you're selling something, you are out of here."

"Fair enough," the man said, stepping into the living room. "I really appreciate this."

Heather closed the door, then turned to look up at Mack Marshall.

This man, she thought, feeling her heart do a strange little two-step, could not possibly be related to Frank. This man was without a doubt the most ruggedly handsome, well-built specimen of the male species she'd ever seen in her twenty-seven years on this earth.

Oh, mercy, look at the square cut of his jaw, the straight blade of his nose, lips that were perfectly proportioned to his other features and…hair. Hair that was thick and black and needed a trim, and eyes that were so dark she could hardly discern the pupils.

His broad shoulders filled out the pale blue dress shirt opened at the neck, and his long, long legs were encased in nice-quality gray slacks, and—

Nope. No way. This Mack Marshall, or whoever he really was, couldn't possibly be Frank's brother, half or otherwise. Frank had been hardly taller than her own five-foot-six, and he'd gained weight just looking at a piece of cake, resulting in a large bulge that covered his belt within a few months of their marriage.

True, Frank had had very dark eyes, but his hair had been brown and thinning. He'd been rather good-looking, in a pleasant, ordinary sense, and he could be extremely charming when the mood struck but—

Heather folded her arms beneath her breasts and tapped one foot.

"The jig is up, Mr. Whoever You Are," she said. "You don't look one bit like Frank Marshall, not even close. I don't know what you're attempting to accomplish here, mister, but it isn't going to work. I'd like you to leave my home. Now."

Mack Marshall raised both hands in a gesture of surrender, then lowered his left hand to his side. He removed his wallet from his back pocket with his right hand and flipped it open.

"Take a look at my identification," he said. "New York driver's license, press card, voter registration, credit cards, the whole nine yards. I *am* Mack Marshall and your late husband was my half brother. I have a folder full of documents in my vehicle if you'd like more proof.''

"Press card?" Heather said. "Wait a minute. Wait just a minute here. Are you saying that you're *the* Mack Marshall, the one who has received a zillion awards for your photographs? You had a book published, too. I read every word when I looked at the book at the library and it was very moving, very... *That* Mack Marshall?"

He smiled. "Guilty."

What he was guilty of, Heather thought, was having a drop-dead smile to go along with his other incredibly masculine attributes. Forget it. That was beside the point. Apparently, Mack really was Frank's half brother and, for reasons yet to be explained, had been determined to find her.

Heather sighed. "I'm being rude and I apologize. Please, have a seat, but it's getting rather late and I have to be up early in the morning. I'd appreciate your explaining as quickly as possible your reasons for going to such lengths to find me."

"Fair enough," he said, nodding.

Mack waited until Heather had settled onto a rocking chair before sitting on the faded sofa opposite her, sweeping his gaze over the room at the same time.

This entire living room, he thought, would fit into the master bathroom in my apartment in New York City. Man, this place is small and shabby. It was clean, though, and he could detect the faint scent of lemon polish. Heather Marshall took pride in her home, such as it was.

And Heather herself? She was lovely, in a wholesome, fresh way. She didn't appear to be wearing any makeup, had very dark eyes and black hair that hung down her back in a thick braid.

Her features were delicate and her figure was slender, well suited to the faded jeans and equally faded T-shirt she was wearing. She was a very pretty woman, his sister-in-law, or was it stepsister-in-law, or ex-stepsister-in-law since she was Frank's widow?

"Why are you staring at me?" Heather said, snapping Mack back to attention.

"Oh. I'm sorry," he said. "I was just trying to figure out what your official title is. You know, sister-in-law, stepsister-in-law. It's not important. What matters is that I've found you at long last."

"Why?" Heather said, frowning. "Why is that important, Mr. Marshall?"

"Mack. Please, call me Mack and I'll call you Heather. After all, we *are* related."

"Back to the question…Mack," Heather said. "Why did you go to such lengths to find me?"

Because he'd nearly died in the dirt halfway around the world, Mack thought, and had been deeply shaken by the fact that he had no family, no one who cared enough to cry at his funeral. That was the truth of the matter, but he wasn't about to bare his soul to a woman he didn't even know.

"I, um, I had some unexpected time on my hands,"

he said, "and I remembered that I had some old boxes that belonged to my father when he was alive. I'd stuck them in storage and forgotten about them for years. When I finally sifted through the stuff, I discovered documents that proved my father had been married briefly before he met my mother. That first marriage produced Frank. For reasons known only to my father, he never told me he'd been married before and had a son older than me.

"I was determined to find Frank. But after weeks of frustration and dead ends, I learned that he was deceased. Then I finally located you and your daughters. And—" Mack shrugged "—here I am."

"Well, that makes sense, I guess," Heather said. "I suppose I'd do the same thing if I suddenly found out I had a relative I hadn't known existed. Except I'm not certain we're actually related, given the circumstances."

"You're a Marshall," Mack said firmly. "That makes us family as far as I'm concerned. My investigation also uncovered that you have no relatives. You, Melissa, Emma and I are it…the full contingent of the Marshall clan."

"You know my daughters' names?" Heather said, her voice rising slightly.

Mack nodded. "And their birthday. I also know your date of birth and…" He frowned. "You don't look exactly thrilled with what I'm saying here."

"Well, my stars," Heather said, throwing up her hands, "how would you feel if a perfect stranger appeared on your doorstep and proceeded to inform you that not only is he a relative of yours, he also knows everything about you? What else did you find out? When I had my last dental appointment? What kind of vehicle I drive? What?''

''Your car is twelve years old,'' Mack said, then cleared his throat. ''I'm sorry, but the information was right in front of me on the computer and—''

''You've invaded my privacy, Mr. Marshall,'' Heather said, ''and I'm going to report you to…to— I don't have the slightest idea who I'm going to report you to. Oh, this is ridiculous.'' She paused. ''Look, I've had a long day and I'm tired. I think it would be best if you left now.''

''May I come back tomorrow?'' Mack said, getting to his feet.

Heather stood and crossed her arms, her hands wrapped around her elbows. ''I really don't see any purpose to be served by it. So, okay, we're related, we're…we're family, if you want to stretch the point. But we come from entirely different worlds. You're a famous photojournalist, a globe-trotting celebrity. I'm a single mother who runs an accounting business out of my home and pinches pennies to provide for my daughters. We have absolutely nothing in common. We've met, said hello, but we have nothing to talk about.''

''What about Frank? I'd like to hear about my half brother.''

"That will take all of sixty seconds," Heather said, rolling her eyes heavenward.

"Heather, I'd really like to meet your daughters, have a chance to get to know them...and you. You're all the family I have and...well, I'm all the family *you* have. Doesn't that mean anything to you?"

"No. Yes. Oh, I don't know," she said, shaking her head. "This is all rather overwhelming. I have to give serious thought to what is best for my daughters. Our family, for all intents and purposes, consists of the people who live on this block.

"I rented this house right after the girls were born and no one has moved away from this street since then. We look out for one another and...I don't want to upset or confuse my daughters by saying, 'Hey, guess what? You have an uncle, or stepuncle, or whatever. Say a quick hello to Mack, girls, before he takes off for parts unknown and we never see him again.' Why disrupt their peaceful and consistent existence like that?"

Heather shook her head. "I'm sorry. You've really thrown me for a loop, and I'm not behaving well. I apologize for being so rude, but I have to think about what is best for my girls."

Mack nodded slowly. "I understand, but perhaps it will help you to reach a decision if I tell you that I won't be doing any traveling for a while. I'm self-employed and I'm on an extended...vacation. I'll definitely be around for a few weeks at least."

"Oh," Heather said. "Don't people in your tax

bracket usually go to more exotic places than Tucson, Arizona, for their vacations?''

''Not when they discover that the only family they have is in Tucson, Arizona,'' Mack said quietly, looking directly into Heather's eyes. ''I want—I *need*—to connect with you and your daughters, Heather. I hope you'll grant me that privilege.''

She couldn't breathe, Heather thought suddenly. The soft, rumbly timbre of Mack's voice, combined with those mesmerizing dark eyes of his, was stealing the very breath from her body.

Mack Marshall was so big, so powerful, so blatantly male, that his very essence seemed to fill the room to overflowing, leaving no space for her, no air to breathe.

Oh, this was frightening, yet somewhere deep within her was a hum of excitement, as well. A heightened awareness of her own femininity as nothing she'd ever experienced before.

No, she didn't want to see Mack again, didn't want him in her home, close to her, unsettling her, throwing her so off kilter. No.

''Heather?'' Mack said. ''May I come back tomorrow? You name the time and I'll be here. Please?''

''Three o'clock,'' Heather heard herself say, then shook her head slightly, stunned at her own response. She sighed in defeat. ''The girls get home from school about two-thirty. I'll explain things to them while we're sharing our snack, then you can arrive and—oh, I hope I'm doing the right thing.''

"You are. Believe me, you are," Mack said, smiling. "Thank you, Heather, more than I can begin to express to you. I'll see you tomorrow afternoon at three o'clock sharp. Good night."

Mack extended his right hand toward Heather and she stared at it for a long moment before placing her right hand in his. He gripped her hand firmly, but didn't release it from his grasp.

"Thank you again," he said.

Heather nodded, told herself to retrieve her hand, but didn't move.

Heat, she registered. There was a strange heat traveling up her arm and across her breasts, causing them to feel heavy and achy, so strange and— She could feel the calluses on Mack's hand, which was so large it totally covered hers. There was power in that hand, but he was holding hers with just the right amount of gentleness and, dear heaven, the heat.

Heather pulled her hand free and hoped Mack didn't see the shuddering breath she took in the next instant.

Mack turned and moved to the door, and Heather followed to lock up behind him.

"Until tomorrow," he said.

"Yes," she said, her voice hardly above a whisper.

Mack left the house and Heather closed and locked the door behind him. She leaned her forehead against the worn wood.

How was it possible, she thought, that a simple knock on the front door could turn her entire world topsy-turvy?

Oh, Heather, stop overreacting, she admonished herself as she spun around and headed for the kitchen to make the almost-forgotten lunches. Anyone would be a tad shaken up to have a stranger suddenly appear on the doorstep and claim to be a long-lost relative.

Her world wasn't topsy-turvy, as her mind had so dramatically described it. It was simply changed a little by the arrival of Mack Marshall. She could handle this. She just needed some rejuvenating sleep, would have this development in its proper perspective in the light of the new day.

"Right," she said dryly as she yanked open the refrigerator door. "If that's true, then why do I have a sneaking suspicion that as of three o'clock tomorrow afternoon my life is never going to be quite the same again?"

Chapter Two

Mack muttered several earthy expletives, tossed back the blankets on the bed, then crossed the room to the large bathroom.

He tore the paper off one of the hotel glasses, filled the glass and swallowed the pill the doctor had prescribed for him when he'd left the hospital in New York City.

He'd been determined to deal with the pain in his shoulder with nothing stronger than aspirin, he fumed, returning to the bed. But he'd been tossing and turning so much, he'd aggravated his wound to the point that he would never be able to sleep with such throbbing pain tormenting him.

Mack sighed and gave himself a firm directive to

relax, turn off his mind and get some much-needed sleep. He was bone-tired and had jet lag, to boot.

His doctor had been none too pleased with Mack's announcement that he was flying to Arizona. The doc had told him that he was far from recovered from the trauma to his body, his energy level was below par, and the wound itself was not totally healed.

Mack had nodded in all the right places as the physician stated his concerns, then told the doctor that the trip could not be postponed any longer and he was leaving the next day.

And here he was, he thought, in the hot, dusty city of Tucson, having accomplished the first step of his mission. He'd met Heather Marshall.

Heather, he mused. Pretty name. Pretty lady. She could, in fact, be stunningly beautiful if she was decked out in an expensive evening dress, had just a touch of makeup on, maybe some glittering jewelry to wear, and allowed her dark hair to tumble down her back in what would be a raven cascade.

Mack frowned into the darkness.

He was mentally transforming Heather into one of the women he was accustomed to dating, one of the wealthy, jet-set gals who wore only the finest and expected to be wined and dined at five-star establishments. He was automatically placing Heather in a social scene where she obviously had never been.

Why was he doing that? Perhaps because it created a sense of familiarity, of knowing what to say to the woman in question, how to flatter her and make her feel special and pampered as she fully expected to be. He was very, very good at that, and the number of women who were always eager to learn that he was once again in New York was proof of that puddin'.

But Heather Marshall? She was from a different world altogether. She lived in a shabby little house in a crummy neighborhood, and wore clothes that had been washed so many times they were nearly void of color.

And she was a mother, for Pete's sake. Did he know any women who were mothers? No, he didn't think he did. What did a guy say to a mother once he'd gushed about how cute her kids were? Hell, what did a man say to six-year-old twin girls?

He really wanted—needed—to connect with Heather and her daughters, but he was so out of his league it was a crime. There had to be something, some common ground he could find. Like…hell, like what?

Mack's frown deepened as he felt a sudden tingling heat in the palm of his right hand, and recalled how delicate and feminine Heather's hand had felt encased in his. He'd been very, very aware of Heather as a woman at that moment, had experienced a jolt of…of lust, he supposed, when he'd held her hand and looked into the depths of her lovely dark eyes.

Ah, now there was a common ground he understood. Good old-fashioned sex, a healthy, physical release. The women he associated with were on the same wavelength on the subject. There were no strings, no commitments. That was how he'd operated his entire adult life, and it had served his purposes just fine, with no complaints from the female contingent.

But there was no way on earth that Heather Marshall operated in that arena. Not a chance. She was hearth, home and motherhood. She probably even baked apple pies.

No, the common ground between him and Heather was not going to be falling into bed together. Even a hint of such a thing would probably get him shot in the other shoulder by the feisty Ms. Marshall.

Man, oh, man, this was complicated. He was determined to cement a family relationship with Heather and her daughters. It had to happen, it just had to. The remembrance of believing he was about to die and realizing no one would give a damn caused a cold fist to tighten in his gut. He never wanted to relive that chilling loneliness. No, never again.

Heather and her girls were his link to having a family, because he sure didn't intend to marry and produce a bunch of kids of his own. No way. He wasn't traveling down that road, thank you very much.

He would firmly establish his role of...of uncle, he guessed. He'd solidify his place in that family unit while he recuperated, then know that the next time he was on the other side of the world he belonged somewhere.

He would know that if he died, Heather and Emma and Melissa would cry.

Was that too much for a man to ask of life? To

know that some people…a family, *his* family, cared? No, he didn't think it was unreasonable, but he'd have to earn that caring somehow.

How was he going to do that when he didn't have a clue how to carry on a conversation with a mother and her children?

The pill Mack had taken began to dull the pain in his shoulder and his mind became fuzzy from the medication and lack of sleep.

He had until three o'clock in the afternoon to figure out how to communicate with Heather and the twins. He'd figure out something…somehow. He was an intelligent man, who just happened…to be…facing a new…challenge, that's all. He'd get…a handle on this. Sure…he would…and he'd do it…by… three…o'clock. Guaranteed.

At last Mack slept, unaware that he'd curled his right hand into a loose fist to hold fast to the warmth of Heather's delicate hand.

Heather sat across from Melissa and Emma at the small table in the kitchen, watching the twins consume their after-school snack of homemade chocolate-chip cookies and glasses of milk.

"And that's the story," Heather said. "Mack Marshall didn't know about us and we didn't know about him. But now he has found us and he'll be here in a few minutes to meet you."

"He doesn't got no kids?" Melissa said, then dunked her cookie into the milk.

"Doesn't *have any* kids. No," Heather said. "We're the only...family he has."

"Mmm," Melissa said, nodding. "Do we have to stay in the house and talk to him for a long bunch of time? Buzzy is coming over so we can play catch."

"Buzzy comes over every day to play catch," Emma said before taking a dainty bite of cookie. "Don't you get tired of throwing a ball back and forth, back and forth, back and forth? You should think of a new game."

"Buzzy an' I need to pra'tice catching with our baseball mitts," Melissa said. "How long do I have to talk to this Mack man, Mom?"

"We'll see how it goes, okay?" Heather said.

"You're not being nice, Melissa," Emma said. "This Mack person is our daddy's brother. That's 'portant."

"Why?" Melissa said. "Our daddy is in heaven, so..." She shrugged.

"Mom," Emma said, "does Mack Marshall look like our daddy did?"

Not even close, sweet Emma, Heather thought as a mental image of Mack flashed in her mind.

"No, not really," Heather said. "Mack and your daddy were half brothers, remember? They had the same father, but not the same mother. That caused them to look very different, so Mack doesn't resemble the picture of your daddy that you have in your bedroom."

"Are we going to 'dopt Mack or something?" Emma said, then patted her lips with her napkin.

Heather's eyes widened. "Adopt him? No, honey, we're just going to get to know him a bit, that's all, because we're related, sort of. He's family, sort of." She paused. "I'm not certain that I'm explaining this very well."

"Sure you are, Mommy," Melissa said. "Mack Marshall doesn't have a family, and found out we're here, and we're his family now, and he's not all alone anymore, and we'll talk to him 'bout dumb stuff like what we want to be when we grow up, then I'll go play catch with Buzzy."

Heather laughed and shook her head. "That's fine, Melissa. I guess that about covers it."

"Poor Mack," Emma said, sighing dramatically. "He's been all alone with no one to talk to for years and years and years. Lots of years, because he's old, right? Really old. You said he's even older than you, Mom. All alone. Poor Mack."

Again an image of Mack took front row center in Heather's mind and an unexpected and very annoying frisson of heat slithered down her back.

"Mack hasn't been all alone, Emma," Heather said. Not a chance. He probably had to carry a big stick to beat off the women who flocked around him. Mack Marshall would be alone only when he chose to be. "I'm sure he has a lot of friends in New York City. In fact, he probably knows people all over the world because he travels a great deal to take photographs."

"That's sure an easy job," Melissa said. "Just take pictures of people. Maybe you should do that, Mom, 'stead of being a 'countant. Then you wouldn't have to work so hard. Can I have another cookie?"

"No, ma'am," Heather said. "That's enough of a snack for after school. I want you to eat a good dinner."

"'Kay," Melissa said. "Well, I'm done with my milk and cookies. When is Mack going to get here?"

Heather glanced at the clock on the wall. "Any minute now. I have a feeling he's going to be right on time."

Mack drove slowly down the street, frowning as he swept his gaze over the small houses that were separated by very narrow driveways.

This neighborhood was even worse than he'd suspected when he'd seen it in the dark last night. Granted, the dozen homes on this dead-end street gave evidence of caring, of making the best of what was available.

But, cripe, these houses were old and so damn small. The only saving grace was the tall mulberry tree in every front yard. But the ancient trees actually made the houses appear even smaller.

He'd driven through some very rundown areas to get here, had seen teenagers hanging out on the corners, many wearing what he had a feeling were gang colors. This entire section of Tucson was crime waiting to happen.

How could Heather sleep at night, knowing she was raising her daughters in such a dangerous location? What kind of a mother would—

Hold it, Marshall. That had been a lousy thing to mentally insinuate about Heather. He was positive that Heather lived here with her girls because this was the best she could afford.

That made sense. The records he'd uncovered about Frank listed his half brother's occupation as a gas station attendant. Not a certified mechanic, just a guy who pumped gas, he guessed. That wouldn't have left any kind of estate to his pregnant widow.

He also knew from his hours on the Internet that Frank Marshall had been killed in an automobile accident driving while drunk. His investigative skills had turned up a copy of the police report. Some more delving had provided the information that the twins had been born about six months later.

Heather Marshall deserved a lot of credit for what she'd done on her own. She'd been young, pregnant, and faced with raising two babies alone. He'd found records of the classes she'd taken for many years, finally obtaining her license as a certified public accountant.

She worked at home, apparently, to be there for her daughters. That meant she had no group medical insurance, no retirement plan, no benefits at all that came from being employed by a large firm.

Hand to mouth, Mack thought, parking in front of

Heather's house. That was how this little family was living. He didn't like that. He sure as hell didn't.

Mack retrieved his parcels from the passenger seat, locked the Blazer he'd rented, then started slowly up the front walk leading to the house. The walkway was cracked in places and several chunks of cement were totally missing.

The minuscule yard was free of weeds, but was more dirt than grass, and a bald tire hung by a rope from a limb on the mulberry tree. The house itself was a rather strange shade of color...not white, not yellow, just dingy gray with no contrasting color on the trim. The roof was a multitude of shades, obviously patched many times over the years with whatever was available.

On the porch, Mack noted the empty hole in the plastic faceplate where the doorbell should have been, and rapped on the door.

He squared his shoulders, took a deep breath and realized to his self-disgust that he was nervous. He, Mack Marshall, who had braved a multitude of dangerous war zones around the globe, was actually shaking in his shorts about the prospect of attempting to carry on a conversation with a mother and her two young daughters. Ridiculous, but annoyingly true.

"Get a grip," he muttered, then waited for the door to open.

"He's here," Melissa said, jumping off her chair. "I'll answer the door."

"No, I want to," Emma said, leaving the table and running after her sister.

"Wait," Heather said, getting to her feet. "Oh, never mind."

She was nervous, she thought, as she trailed after the girls. She'd had a difficult time concentrating on her work while the twins were in school, had glanced at the clock so often she'd felt like one of those bobbing toys that people put on the dashboards of their cars. Ridiculous.

As Heather heard a chorus of, "Hi. Come in," she smoothed the waistband of her bright red string sweater over her jeans-clad hips and produced what she hoped was a believable smile.

"Hello, Mack," she said as he stepped into the living room.

Oh, gracious, she thought, Mack was even better looking today than he had been last night. How was that possible? But Mack Marshall in black slacks and a navy-blue knit shirt was a sight to behold.

Her heart was beating too fast. What was wrong with her heart? Why was it doing that? Forget it. Just forget it. She had to act like a mature adult, a mother, for heaven's sake.

"I'd like you to meet my daughters." She placed one hand on Emma's shoulder. "This is Emma." The other hand plopped onto Melissa's head. "And this is Melissa. Girls, this is Mack Marshall. Your…your uncle. Yes, that's what you can call him…Uncle Mack."

"Hi," the pair said in unison.

"Hi," Mack said, staring at them.

They were *identical* twins, he thought incredulously. They both had short, curly black hair, big dark eyes, the very same features and—he'd never been face-to-face with identical twins before.

They were wearing different clothes, thank goodness, which would help him to keep them straight. Emma was wearing a flowered dress and Melissa was decked out in jeans and a baseball jersey that was a bit too big for her.

"I brought you a little something." Mack handed Heather a bouquet of spring flowers, then gave each of the girls an enormous cellophane-wrapped, rainbow-colored sucker.

"Wow," Melissa said. "I've never seen a sucker this big. This is so cool. Can I eat it now, Mom?"

"I'm going to save mine forever," Emma said. "It's so pretty. I've never had such a big, beautiful sucker."

"What do you say?" Heather said.

"Thank you," the twins chorused.

"And I thank you for the lovely flowers, Mack," Heather said, not looking directly at him. "Please, have a seat while I put these in water. And, Melissa, no, you can't have any candy now. We'll decide after dinner how much of it you can eat at one time. I'll be right back."

Heather hurried from the room. Once safely in the kitchen and out of view, she buried her face in the lovely flowers and inhaled their sweet aroma.

Oh, darn, she thought frantically, she could feel the sting of tears. She had to get a grip, regain control of her emotions now. *Right now.* It was just that she had never, not once in her entire life, been given flowers by a man. She felt like Emma...she wanted to keep them forever.

Heather opened a cupboard, remembered that she didn't own a vase, then proceeded to half fill an empty pickle jar with water and arrange the flowers. She returned to the living room and placed the makeshift vase on the coffee table.

Mack was sitting on the sofa with a twin on each side of him, each holding their sucker and staring up at him.

He looked about as comfortable as a man waiting to have a root canal, Heather thought, curbing a smile as she seated herself in the rocker. She had the distinct impression that Mack's experience with children was zip.

"So," Heather said, "are you enjoying our weather, Mack? March is a lovely month here, and April will be even nicer." Good grief, was this the best she could do? Talk about the weather? But *her* experience in conversing with a worldly man such as Mack was most definitely zip. "I've told the girls that you're a famous photographer."

"Well, yes, I do take pictures of...of things," he said, glancing at Melissa, then Emma. "Lots and lots of photographs."

"Where's your camera?" Melissa said.

"It's locked in my vehicle out front," Mack said. "I never go anywhere without it, it seems. Would you like me to take your picture?"

"No," Melissa said.

"Oh," he said, then cleared his throat.

"Do you have a house?" Emma said.

"A house? No, I have an apartment that I rent in New York City. I'm not there too much of the time, though, because I travel a great deal taking photographs."

"Oh-h-h," Emma said, nodding. "We rent our house, too, but we have a dream piggy. Maybe if you got a real job, instead of just playing with a camera and stuff, you could get a dream piggy, too, and get a house."

"Emma," Heather said quickly, "being a photojournalist is a real job, a very difficult one, in fact. Mack has won a great many awards with his photographs."

"But Uncle Mack doesn't have enough money to buy a house, Mommy," Emma said. "He needs a dream piggy."

"What's a dream piggy, Emma?" Mack asked.

"Well." Emma set the sucker very carefully next to her on the sofa, then folded her hands in her lap. "You see, when you want something more than anything else in the whole wide world...that's your dream. Me and Melissa and my mommy want to have our very own house, buy it, not rent it and everything, and fix it up real nice, and have enough bedrooms for everyone to have their very own, and we save all our pennies and stuff in our dream piggy, 'cause someday we're going to have our dream. Our house. Get it?''

Mack nodded slowly. "Got it."

"So!" Emma continued. "You could get a house, too, but you gotta have a dream piggy first so you have a place to put your pennies."

"I'll certainly give that some serious thought," Mack said. "I appreciate your telling me about a dream piggy, Emma. I didn't know such a thing existed."

Emma's eyes widened. "You didn't? Wow. Well, now you know, so that's okay."

"Not everyone has the same dream, Emma," Heather said. "Maybe Mack doesn't want to own a house."

"Buzzy doesn't care if he has a house," Melissa said. "His dream is to be the bestest baseball player in the whole wide world."

"What's your dream, Uncle Mack?" Emma said, gazing up at him.

"I, um, well, Emma, I..." Mack stopped speaking and sent a pleading look at Heather, who just smiled at him pleasantly. "I guess I don't have a dream."

Emma's little hands flew to her cheeks. "You don't? Oh, that's terrible. That's really, really terrible. My mommy says that dreams are 'portant, 'cause they're magic, and they help you work harder and never give up no matter what, and...and stuff. Right, Mommy?"

"That's right, Emma," Heather said, smiling at her warmly.

Emma reached over and patted Mack on the knee, causing him to jerk in surprise.

"Don't worry, Uncle Mack," Emma said, "we'll help you find a dream for yourself. Okay? We will. I promise. So don't be sad that you don't have a dream right now, 'cause we're going to fix that. If it's the kind of dream that needs pennies, we'll need to get you a dream piggy, too." She patted Mack's knee again. "Just don't be sad. Okay?"

A strange warmth along with a foreign achiness in his throat suffused Mack as he looked at Emma and saw the sincere concern on her little face. He nodded, not certain he was capable of speaking at that moment.

A loud knock sounded at the front door and again Mack jerked in surprise.

"Buzzy," Heather, Melissa and Emma said in unison.

"Can I go play ball now, Mommy?" Melissa said. "Please?"

"Yes, you may," Heather said. "You know the rules. You stay in our front yard, or Buzzy's."

"'Kay." Melissa slid off the sofa, placed her sucker on the coffee table next to the pickle jar holding the flowers, then ran to the front door, flinging it open. "Hi, Buzzy. I'll get my mitt. Guess what? We got a new uncle, who didn't know we were here, but now he does, and he brought me the biggest sucker that was ever made."

"Cool," a voice said. "Can I have a lick of your sucker?"

"Maybe. I'll be right back."

Melissa ran across the room, down the hall, then returned moments later with an obviously very worn baseball mitt.

"Melissa," Heather said as the little girl zoomed past her. "Say goodbye to Uncle Mack."

"'Bye," Melissa said, then left the house, yanking the door closed behind her.

Emma wiggled off the sofa and picked up her sucker. "I'm going to put this in a special safe place in my part of the bedroom, Mom. I'm keeping it forever, you know."

Heather glanced quickly at the flowers. "Yes, Emma, I know."

"'Bye, Uncle Mack," Emma said. "Don't forget now. We're gonna help you find your dream."

"I won't forget," Mack said, smiling at her. "And I thank you for that, Emma, I really do."

"No-o-o-o problem," Emma said, then left the room, cradling the sucker in her arms as though it were a baby doll. Mack took a deep breath and let it out slowly, puffing his cheeks and shaking his head.

"I'm exhausted," he said, chuckling. "That was the most amazing conversation I've ever taken part in in my entire life." He paused. "Heather, your daughters are wonderful, absolutely fantastic."

"Thank you," she said, dipping her head slightly. "I rather like them myself."

"But how do you keep up with them? I mean, their minds never stop, and they're so honest and real, just tell it like it is. They're completely different, aren't they? Even though they're identical twins their personalities are like day and night."

"Oh, yes," Heather said, laughing. "Emma is very ladylike and tries to be so prim and proper all the time, and Melissa is my tomboy. They do keep me on my toes. I love them so much, Mack. I simply can't imagine my life without them."

"Mmm," Mack said, nodding. "It would seem that I'm to have assistance in getting a dream for myself."

"Well, be forewarned that Emma won't forget about that. Once she gets something in her mind, it's there to stay until she deals with it." Heather frowned. "You really don't have any hopes and dreams?"

"Until today," Mack said, "I never thought about it. But, well, no, I guess I don't."

"Just humor Emma for a while on the subject," Heather said. "We place a great deal of emphasis on our dream to have our own home. I realize now that Emma and Melissa assume that everyone has, or should have, a dream, too, but I have to admit that I agree with that philosophy."

"Why?"

"Because a dream gives you a purpose, a goal, a whimsical sense of a magical time yet to come. A dream provides hope when you're trying to survive, just make it day to day."

Heather sighed. "Never mind, Mack. I'm not certain you can understand all this, because your lifestyle is so very different from ours. If you want something, I imagine you can go out and buy it as the mood strikes.''

''Well...''

''Please don't think I'm doing an oh-poor-us routine here, because I'm not. It's just that we're from such different worlds that I'm not certain we can connect on any level. That wouldn't be your fault, nor mine, it would just be the way things are. You're welcome to visit us, if you choose, while you're on vacation here in Tucson, but I don't expect we'll find a common ground while you're in town.''

''Oh, that's not true, Heather,'' Mack said, looking directly at her. ''We've already connected on a couple of things.''

''Such as?''

''Your daughters have staked a claim on my heart that feels great. It really does. I may grow old before my time just trying to keep up with them during a conversation, but I like them very, very much.''

''Well, that's one,'' Heather said, smiling. ''You said a *couple* of things.''

Mack nodded. ''It's come to light that I don't have a dream, and this—'' he swept his right arm through the air ''—is the place where I'm going to get the help I need to find one.''

Chapter Three

The next afternoon Buzzy's mother, Susie Jenkins, and Heather were in a used-clothing store, sifting through the jumble of merchandise on a large table. Melissa, Emma and Buzzy were playing in the corner of the shop, building a tower from wooden blocks.

Heather held up a T-shirt with a smiling Garfield on the front. "Melissa." The next item she found was a pink top boasting a cute gray kitten with a white bow around its neck. "Emma."

"Buzzy," Susie said, showing Heather a shirt with a multicolored dinosaur.

"We're on a roll," Heather said, laughing. "The last time we were in here we came up empty."

"Keep digging through the goodies," Susie said,

"but don't stop with the story. What you haven't told me is whether or not you like this Mack Marshall who showed up on your doorstep."

"He's...nice," Heather said with a shrug. "It's a little early to say whether or not I like him as a person, because I don't really know him. I got all choked up because he brought me flowers, but that was silly of me. It was a lovely gesture on his part and no one has ever given me flowers before and—

"I think Mack is very sincere in his desire to get to know Melissa, Emma and me, to feel connected to a family...his family...us. I'm not sure why he's determined to do that, but I believe he means what he says about wanting to do it."

"Maybe it's because he was shot and nearly died," Susie said, holding a pair of jeans at arm's length. "Too short. You know, his life passed before his eyes and—"

"Shot?" Heather interrupted. "Mack didn't say anything about being hurt."

"I read it in the newspaper at the library," Susie said. "He was in...oh, I forget where...some war-torn country doing his photojournalist thing and he got shot. It happened about a month or two ago. I'm surprised he's well enough already to be winging his way out here to meet you. They showed a file picture of him along with the article. Heather, that is one dreamy-looking guy."

"Where was he shot?" Heather said.

"I told you. In some remote place—"

"No, no, I mean, on his...person. He wasn't limping or anything. I mean, shot?"

Susie narrowed her eyes. "I think...yes, it was his shoulder, his left shoulder. He was saving an old couple from the rebel gunfire and—pow—Mack Marshall got shot. It took forever to get him the help he needed way out there, but the article said he was finally recuperating in a hospital in New York City."

"He said he was on vacation," Heather said, forgetting to look at the clothes.

"Well, gee whiz, Heather," Susie said, "it wouldn't be very macho for him to sit in your living room and go on and on about his boo-boo."

"Getting shot is not a boo-boo, Susie," Heather said, none too quietly.

"Who got shot, Mommy?" Melissa yelled from the play area.

"We're just talking about a movie, Melissa," Heather said.

"Oh." Melissa placed another block on the teetering tower.

"Heather Marshall," Susie said, laughing. "You just lied to your very own child. Shame on you."

"I can't tell the girls that Mack was shot," Heather said. "It's too violent, harsh, and they don't really need to know."

"Whatever," Susie said. "But why are you so shook up about Mack Marshall being hurt? He obviously didn't die. But I betcha when he thought he was going to buy the farm, he realized he didn't have any family to bury him. It makes sense, don't you think? He dug up the info on your husband, discovered you and the girls existed even though his half brother is deceased and—ta-da—he's here in Tucson.''

''Yes, it does make sense,'' Heather said, ''but it's rather disconcerting, Susie.''

''Why?''

''Well, I figured he was just bored. He'd gone through his father's belongings, was curious about the half brother he never knew he had and wasn't in the mood to lounge on an exotic beach somewhere so he came here to hang around for a few weeks. But...shot? That changes everything.''

''You've totally lost me,'' Susie said. ''Oh, hey, look at this frilly dress. Emma would love this.''

''Thanks,'' Heather said, absently placing the dress in the pile of clothes she intended to buy. ''Susie, listen to me. If Mack wants to be part of our family because he nearly died and realized he didn't have anyone to call his own, that puts a tremendous burden on me and the girls. We have to be for Mack what he *needs* us to be, don't you see? He's not just filling idle hours, the man is on a very focused mission.''

''So?'' Susie said. ''What's the problem with his wanting to be part of your family?''

''We have nothing in common. Nothing. Mack is rich, he's famous, he's a celebrity. Yes, I think he sincerely wants to know he has a family, but I figured once he spent a little time with us, he'd go merrily on his way, satisfied that he'd found his long-lost relatives. But if he's wanting, needing, to really bond with us because he nearly died, it isn't going to work.''

"You think he'll leave and go back to being a jet-setting playboy,'' Susie said.

"Oh, yes, he'll leave, but I'm worried about the girls," Heather said. "What if…somehow…they get the impression that we didn't measure up to Mack's standards? My girls are not dumb. It isn't going to take many more conversations for them to realize that their uncle Mack is from a world far removed from ours. I will not allow my daughters to feel inferior in any way, shape or form, just because we don't have a lot of money.''

"Heather," Susie said, "I don't think that Mack would do anything to make his newfound family feel inferior, for heaven's sake. Besides, he's with you on *your* turf, in *your* home, *your* neighborhood. Did he rave on and on about his house in New York City?''

"Well, no," Heather said, "he just said he rented an apartment, and Emma told him he needed a dream piggy so he could save his pennies to buy himself a house.''

Susie laughed. "I love it. Oh, Heather, you're worrying about nothing. Mack is recuperating from a gunshot wound. He'll get better, then be on his way, knowing he has a family in sunny Tucson, Arizona. You'll probably get a Christmas card from him in the future, and that will be that. The girls aren't going to come to any harm by spending some time with the man.''

"I suppose you're right," Heather said, frowning. "But I'm definitely going to stay on alert whenever we're with him. I'll make certain the conversations don't get centered somehow on how much money Mack has, the kind of lifestyle he enjoys, anything like that."

Heather sighed. "Listen to me. Do you hear what I'm doing? I'm scared, Susie, that my daughters will look at me and want to know why we live like we do, when their uncle Mack, who is part of our family now, has so much more than we do. The problem isn't with Mack Marshall, it's with me."

Susie put one arm around Heather's shoulders. "I think you're hitting the nail on the head, sweetie. As the teenagers say, 'Get over it.' You're doing a wonderful job raising the girls and you should be very proud of what you've accomplished. Don't be so sensitive about what Mack has and you don't. Just enjoy his company when you're together and before you know it, he'll be gone. When are you supposed to see him again?"

"He's taking us out for pizza tonight."

"Oh, wow," Susie said, "the guy is really throwing his bucks around, the rotten bum. Give Mack Marshall a little credit here, why don't you? He's not going to attempt to change your lifestyle, or stand in judgment of it, he just wants to be a part of it for a little while. Hey, send him over to my house. That hunk of stuff can eat crackers in my bed any night of the week."

"Susie!" Heather said with a burst of laughter.

"Yeah, well, unlike you, my dear, I am not averse to marrying again. This single mother jazz is the pits. Buzzy needs a father and I need a lover. So there. I wish Mack Marshall was a long-lost relative of mine, let me tell you. You're not biologically related, you know, so you two could—"

"Don't even think about it," Heather said, frowning. "I'm not interested in Mack as a man. He's uncle to my girls and I'm not even comfortable with that for the reasons I've stated.

"Yes, yes, I know, I'm the one with the problem about the differences in our tax brackets. But my girls consider the people on our little block their family, and we're all in the same financial leaky boat. I'll be glad when Mack leaves town and the girls and I can get back to living our nice, normal lives as we were, putting pennies in our dream piggy."

"Unfortunately, that will happen all too soon, I'd guess," Susie said. "Once Mack's shoulder heals he'll be long gone."

"Amen to that." Heather rolled her eyes heavenward. "I put the flowers he gave me in a pickle jar that still had the label on it, for crying out loud. Nothing like advertising to the oh-so-rich uncle of my daughters that I don't even own a vase."

"Forget it," Susie said, wrinkling her nose. "Men don't notice things like that. No way. Forget about the pickle jar. Mack never saw it."

A pickle jar, Mack thought as he wandered through the large, enclosed shopping mall. Heather had put the flowers he'd brought her in a crummy pickle jar, for heaven's sake. If she'd had a pretty vase, she would have used it. How was it she didn't even own a vase for flowers?

Mack frowned and shook his head as he continued his trek through the mall. He stopped in front of a toy store and swept his gaze over the display in the window.

He was taking Heather and the twins out for pizza tonight, he mused. Heather had hesitated when he asked if they'd like to go to dinner so he'd quickly tacked on the idea of a casual pizza parlor, which she'd agreed to.

That meant, he was guessing, that Heather felt she and her daughters didn't own fancy enough clothes to dine at a high-class restaurant.

And there he sat in Heather's shabby little living room wearing slacks, shoes and a shirt that probably cost more than the sofa he'd been sitting on.

This whole scenario was wrong, very wrong. He was no expert on the dynamics of family, that was for damn sure, but the Heather branch of the Marshall clan had relatively nothing, while the Mack branch had more money than he could spend in a lifetime. He made big bucks and had invested well, could retire today if he wanted to...which he didn't...but...

It wasn't supposed to be like this, was it? A family didn't consist of those who had and those who didn't. Did it? Cripe, he didn't know. He hadn't paid the least bit of attention to the family structures of the people he knew. Not that he knew a lot of people who had families.

Oh, man, he was confusing himself to the point that he was tensing up and his shoulder was killing him. He needed a crash course on how to be part of a family, how to behave, what his role was, the whole bit.

Well, forget it, because that kind of information wasn't readily available. He'd have to wing it. Yep, that was all he could do. He'd pay attention, try to figure out how to be a good uncle to the girls and a...a what to Heather? A brother?

The sudden vision of Heather's lovely, smiling face caused a flash of heat to rocket through his body.

Nope. Brother wasn't going to cut it, not even close. Granted, he'd already realized that hustling Heather into bed was not on the agenda. No way. But act like her brother? That was too far out in left field. Besides, he didn't have any experience in being anyone's brother, either.

So, okay, he'd be her... What? Her friend? Her buddy? Her pal? That wasn't it. No. Heather was family. That still didn't give him a clue as to how he should act around her.

He was just going to have to get very basic here. He was a man. Heather was a woman. He'd treat her with the respect she deserved and let the chips fall where they may. He'd keep his hands to himself and watch for any signals from Heather that she might be

interested in him not just as a long-lost relative who
had suddenly appeared in her life.

Yes, that was the ticket. Let Heather call the shots.
If he ended up acting like her big brother—as nause-
ating as that thought was—so be it. He would do nothing to jeopardize his place in that little family. Nothing.

In the meantime, he thought, pulling open the door
to the toy shop, Uncle Mack was going to get a surprise for those cute-as-a-button little girls. He had a
handle on their personalities now, could do a lot better
than showing up with candy suckers.

And, by damn, he was going to see to it that Heather
Marshall never again had to put pretty flowers in a
pickle jar.

Just before six o'clock that night Heather stood in
front of the full-length mirror mounted on the back of
her bedroom door.

She looked, she decided, presentable for going out
for pizza. She'd French-braided her hair, which gave
it a bit more style than just her usual plait. Her navy-
blue slacks were fine, the place where she mended
them covered by the blue-flowered overblouse. She'd
even polished her loafers until they shone.

Heather sighed and sank onto the edge of the bed.

She wanted this evening to be over before it had
even begun. She was nervous, unsettled, did *not* want
to spend the following hours in the company of Mack
Marshall.

Talking to Susie had helped her to sort through some of her jumbled thoughts. It had been months, even years, since she'd scrutinized how well she was providing for the girls. Melissa and Emma were happy, well-adjusted children, who never questioned their lifestyle, who believed in hopes and wishes, who put pennies in a piggy toward their ultimate dream of living in their very own house.

Her daughters had an extended family made up of the kind and loving people on this block. Melissa and Emma knew they were welcome in those homes, cared about, could go to any neighbor and get a hug, a Band-Aid or a drink of water if they needed it.

And now? In waltzes a *real* family member. The famous, rich-beyond-measure Mack Marshall, and his emergence into their lives was terrifying. Mack didn't wear used clothing, nor live in a tiny little house. Mack didn't have to pinch pennies, nor save them in a piggy. Mack could have anything he wanted just by writing a check or pulling out his wallet or producing a credit card.

If we're all part of the same family, Mommy, why does Uncle Mack have so much and we have nothing? That's not fair, Mommy, it's not. How come we don't have a bunch of stuff, Mommy—

"Stop," Heather whispered to the voices in her head, pressing her fingertips to her now-throbbing temples.

Susie was right. Mack was on *their* turf, would sit in the living room of *their* home. Her twins, who couldn't help but make comparisons, wouldn't see what Mack had to be able to question what they didn't possess.

Right?

Oh, dear heaven, she hoped so. It would break her heart if her children became unhappy, began to yearn for what never could be, saw their life and, thus, themselves, as being less than what they should be.

"Mack Marshall, go home," Heather said out loud, getting to her feet. "Just go home and leave us alone."

Oh, that was awful. Mack wanted, needed, to be part of a family, even for a short while as he recuperated from being shot. Shot, for mercy's sake. What kind of a human being was she to be wishing he'd never shown up to stake a claim on his rightful place in their family unit? Tacky. Very tacky.

So, okay, she'd get through this. Mack didn't intend to stay in Tucson very long, only a couple of weeks. She'd just treat him like a...a...what? Brother?

Heather looked at her right hand and remembered the incredible heat that had traveled up her arm and across her breasts when Mack held that hand in his strong but gentle one.

Brother was *not* going to work.

So, okay, they were...simply members of the same family...sort of. They were half ex-whatever-they-were people who...

Oh, who was she kidding? Mack was the most blatantly sensuous man she had ever met in her entire life. And she was a woman, a fact she'd rather forgotten, or taken for granted, until Mack Marshall had made her so acutely aware of her own femininity.

This, Heather thought, pointing one finger in the air, was *not* good. The mere thought of Mack caused her heart to do a funny little two-step and that disturbing heat to travel throughout her entire body.

Mack Marshall was...was—oh, hey, she had it now—he was Melissa's and Emma's uncle. There. That title was perfect. It meant thinking of him in terms of the girls rather than thinking about the disconcerting effect he had on her as a man.

"Uncle Mack is here," Melissa yelled from the front door.

And so are the butterflies, Heather thought in self-disgust as she placed one hand on her stomach and made her way to the living room.

"He's coming up the walk," Melissa announced, then began to jump up and down. "And he's got presents. He's got presents with him, Mom."

Heather narrowed her eyes and quickened her step to get to the door.

"Hi, Uncle Mack," Melissa said after opening the front door. "Do you like my new shirt? It's Garfield. See? I just got it today, and we washed it and stuff so I could wear it to go out for pizza, and Emma got a new dress, and we washed that too and Mom had to iron it 'cause it was all wrinkly, but she didn't have to iron my Garfield. Aren't you going to come into the house?"

"He can't because you're standing in his way, sweetheart," Heather said.

"Oh," Melissa said, stepping back.

Mack entered the living room just as Emma came running to join the group.

"Hi, Uncle Mack," Emma said, stopping in front of him. "Oh, you've got presents. Is it your birthday? Are you going to open your birthday presents so we can see what you got?"

"No," Mack said, smiling. "It's not my birthday. These gifts are for you, and your sister, and your mother."

Emma frowned. "It's not *our* birthdays."

"We're celebrating that fact that it's Friday," Mack said.

"Why?" Emma asked.

"Why?" Mack repeated. "Well, because that means there's no school for the next two days, which leaves you free to play, and that is something to celebrate."

"It is?" Emma said. "I didn't know that."

"Uncle Mack just made it up for fun," Heather said, looking at Mack intently. "You girls like school as much as you do playing on the weekend. Right?"

"I guess," Melissa said, shrugging.

"Right, Mack?" Heather said, narrowing her eyes.

"Oh. Right. Sure. You bet," he said, nodding. "I was just kidding. These gifts I brought are simply because I'm very glad to see all of you." He handed one of the presents to Emma, another to Melissa, then extended a brightly wrapped gift toward Heather. "This one is for you, Heather."

"Mack," Heather said, accepting the package, "I really wish you hadn't…"

"Can I open it, Mommy?" Melissa said, jumping up and down again. "Can I? Please?"

"May I," Heather said absently, then sighed. "Yes, of course, go ahead and open your surprises."

The girls sat on the floor and tore away the pretty paper.

"Oh! Oh! Oh!" Melissa said, popping up to her feet again. "It's a new baseball mitt. Look at this, Mommy. It's a brand-new baseball mitt." She flung her arms around Mack and gave him a big hug. "Thank you, thank you, thank you. Can I go show Buzzy my new mitt, Mom?"

"No, honey," Heather said quietly, "there isn't time now. We're going out for pizza, remember? You can show it to Buzzy in the morning."

"'Kay." Melissa pressed the mitt to her nose. "It smells so good. Oh, this is the bestest present I ever got in my whole life."

"Oh-h-h," Emma said after she'd unwrapped her gift. "A Barbie doll. A real Barbie doll." She held it tightly, then got to her feet and hugged Mack. "Thank you, Uncle Mack. My Barbie doll is so beautiful. She's the most beautiful doll I've ever had since I was borned."

Mack chuckled. "Well, I'm glad you both like what I picked out for you. That makes me feel great, it really does." He looked at Heather. "Aren't you going to open your present?"

No, Heather thought, she wasn't going to open her

gift, she was going to run to her bedroom and cry for a week. Her worst nightmare was already happening. Her daughters had just declared the expensive gifts from Mack to be the very best presents they had ever received. A brand-new baseball mitt that smelled like the genuine leather that it was and a gorgeous Barbie doll. Brand-new...not used by someone else before the twins.

"Mommy?" Melissa said. "Aren't you going to open your present?"

"What?" she said. "Oh, yes, of course, I am." Heather sat on the sofa and a few moments later lifted a delicate crystal vase from the tissue paper inside the box. "Oh, my goodness. It's...it's lovely. I've never had anything so..." She cleared her throat. "Thank you very much, Mack."

"Cool," Melissa said. "Now you won't have to put flowers in the pickle jar."

"That's the plan," Mack said.

So much for Mack not noticing the dumb pickle jar, Heather thought miserably. And she had gushed over her gift just as much as the girls had...and she'd meant it. The vase was exquisite. And it probably cost more than she spent on a week's worth of groceries.

"Get your sweaters, girls," Heather said, placing the vase on the coffee table. "It will be chilly once the sun goes down."

"Can I take my mitt with me to the pizza parlor?" Melissa said.

"Can I take my Barbie doll?" Emma said.

"Sure," Heather said wearily as she got to her feet. "Why not? Run and get your sweaters."

The twins ran from the room and Heather turned to look at Mack.

"I will never," he said quietly, "forget what just took place here. I wish I could have captured on film the pure and innocent joy on those girls' faces when they opened their presents. How can I thank you, Heather, for allowing me to be here, to be a part of this family, to witness such incredibly honest happiness?"

Oh, drat, Heather thought. She had been ready to deliver a stern lecture to Mack about not having asked her permission to bring the girls such expensive gifts and to tell him not, absolutely not, to do it again.

But how could she do that now? There stood Mack Marshall, choking up with emotion over the reactions of the twins to his presents. She'd be rotten to the core if she destroyed this moment for him.

"I'm glad you like your vase," Mack said. "We all received gifts here this evening. I know I'm going to cherish the memory of mine."

Heather produced a small smile as the girls came running back into the room.

"Let's go eat pizza," Heather said.

"Wait, wait," Melissa said. "Mommy, you didn't hug Uncle Mack to thank him for your flower vase."

"Oh, well, I..." Heather said, feeling a flush of embarrassment stain her cheeks.

Mack opened his arms. "Melissa's right."

Heather looked at the twins, who were looking at

her, then stared at a spot in the center of Mack's chest as she stepped forward into his embrace.

She fluttered her hands in the air for a moment, not quite certain what to do with them, then finally splayed them lightly on Mack's back.

He was powerful and solid and warm, Heather thought. It had been years since she'd been held in a man's strong and protective embrace. It felt so good, so—oh, gracious, it felt *too* good and she was ending this thank-you-for-the-vase hug right now. Well, maybe in another moment or two...or four...or— She was being consumed by a scorching heat that was sweeping through her and, dear heaven, what was happening to her?

Heather jerked, bumping Mack's left shoulder in the process, and felt him stiffen.

"Oh, I'm so sorry," she said, stepping back. "Did I hurt you? I know it hasn't been that long since you were shot and I—"

"Shot?" Melissa said, her eyes widening. "With a gun? Some bad guy shot you, Uncle Mack? That's terrible, just awful. You aren't going to die, are you? Please, Uncle Mack, please don't die." She burst into tears. "I don't want you to die the way our daddy did."

"Melissa, honey," Heather said, "calm down. Uncle Mack isn't going to die. He—"

"No, no, no," Emma said, sniffling. "He won't die. He can't die. He just found us and he's part of our family now and we get to keep him forever. Right, Mommy? Please, Mommy?"

"Whoa," Mack said. "I'm not going to die. I was hurt—okay, I was shot while I was taking pictures in a dangerous place, but I'm going to be fine. I just need a little more time for my wound to heal, that's all. There's nothing to worry about."

"Promise?" Melissa said.

"I promise," Mack said.

"And we get to keep you forever and ever, Uncle Mack?" Emma said.

"I—" Mack started.

"Oh, gracious, look at the time," Heather said. "If we don't get going, there will be a huge crowd at the pizza parlor. Off we go. Be thinking about what kind of pizza you want, girls. Oops. I need to get my sweater, too. I'll meet you all out front."

As the trio left the house, Heather hurried to her bedroom and snatched up her sweater from the bed.

Do we get to keep you forever and ever, Uncle Mack? her mind echoed. No, sweet Emma, they wouldn't get to keep Mack forever and ever. He'd be leaving soon and they'd probably never see him again. He'd be leaving soon and their lives would return to normal.

Yes, Mack Marshall would be leaving soon, and she knew without a doubt that when he left, she would miss him for a very long time.

Chapter Four

The pizza parlor was crowded and noisy, but the four Marshalls managed to find an empty booth. A discussion immediately ensued regarding what toppings should be on their pizza.

"Just cheese," Emma said. "No other goop. Just cheese."

"No way," Melissa said. "It should have everything 'cept those little fishy things."

"Yuck," Emma said. "I only like cheese on my pizza, Melissa, and you know it." She folded her arms over her chest and leaned back in the booth, glaring at her sister. "I don't want to have to pick all that junk off so I can eat my cheese."

"Aren't they charming?" Heather said, smiling at Mack. "Ah, sisterly love."

"And what do *you* like on your pizza, Heather?" Mack said.

"Anything," Heather said, shrugging. "Everything." She laughed. "But not those little fishy things."

"Okay," Mack said, nodding. "This is easily solved. Moving right along...what about drinks?"

"Can we have soda, Mom?" Melissa said. "Please? Please? Please?"

"Yes, all right," Heather said. "Going out for pizza is a very special treat, so we might as well go for the gusto. You may have soda."

"Yes," Melissa said, punching one fist in the air.

"You shouldn't do that, Melissa," Emma said. "You're going to hit somebody right in the nose."

"I am not," Melissa said.

"That's enough, girls," Heather said. "Uncle Mack doesn't want to hear you squabbling any more than I do, so stop it right now."

"'Kay," Melissa said. "Sorry."

"Sorry," Emma said, "but it better not be my nose Melissa hits."

Mack laughed. "Mine, either. I'm off to order the pizzas. Melissa, Emma, try not to do bodily harm to each other while I'm gone."

"Let's color our place mats, Emma," Melissa said, reaching for a basket of crayons on the table. "I'll let you have the red first."

"'Kay," Emma said.

"Thank you, girls. That's much better behavior,"

Heather said absently as she watched Mack make his way across the crowded room.

Heavens, she thought, the women in this place were practically falling off their chairs to get a good look at Mack. He didn't seem to be paying the least bit of attention to the female gawkers, though. He was probably used to being given second, third and fourth approving glances. And with just cause.

Well, too bad, ladies, because Mack Marshall was taken for the evening. He was with her. Well, with the twins too but... They appeared, she supposed, to be a family—Mom, Dad, and cute twin daughters. They all had the same black hair and dark eyes and—yes, they most definitely looked like a family who had decided to go out for pizza on a Friday night.

Heather sighed.

That was how it should have been, how she'd hoped and dreamed it would be when she'd married Frank. She'd envisioned being part of a loving couple, then later there would be children born of that love. That dream had been shattered so quickly, it was as though it had never existed in her heart, mind and soul.

"Can I have the red now, Emma?" Melissa said.

"Sure," she said, handing over the crayon.

Heather shifted her gaze to her daughters and smiled. Their heads were bent over their place mats, each paying careful attention to their coloring.

All the tears she'd shed, when she discovered that Frank was not the man she'd thought him to be were worth it tenfold. Her broken heart had been put back together by the birth of her two little miracles, Emma and Melissa. Just looking at them made it easy to understand why Mack wanted to bond with his newfound family.

Please, Uncle Mack, please don't die. I don't want you to die the way our daddy did. He can't die. He just found us and he's part of our family now and we get to keep him forever. Right, Mommy? Please, Mommy?

Oh, dear, Heather thought, pressing her fingertips to her temples. She had to talk to Mack. Between them they had to remind the girls that Mack would be leaving soon, slip in that fact whenever conversation made it feasible.

The twins were becoming very fond of Mack very quickly. They didn't want to lose him the way they'd lost the father they had never even known. They wanted their mommy to tell them that they could keep Uncle Mack forever, and that yearning had to be nipped in the bud. She didn't want her daughters' hearts to be broken when Mack left Tucson.

And *your* heart, Heather? she asked herself. When she'd hugged Mack to thank him for the beautiful vase, she'd been struck by a sense of being where she belonged, encircled in his strong, protective arms. And she'd felt that heat again, that raging, burning heat of what she knew was desire, of a woman wanting a man, wanting to make love with that man. Wanting Mack.

Stop it, she admonished herself. This was ridiculous. She hardly knew Mack Marshall, but there she sat, admitting that she desired him, wanted him. That was terrible, and frightening and—

Well, it made sense in a way. It had been many years since she'd been held by a man, made to feel special and pretty and feminine.

It wasn't Mack, she told herself, it was simply the fact that he was there, close to her, nudging awake her womanliness that had been slumbering for a very long time.

It was basic biological urges, and had nothing to do with Mack the man.

Yes, of course, she'd miss Mack when he left. What woman wouldn't? That would be a normal reaction. But within a short while after Mack left, she and the girls would be back to their routine and the memories of the time spent with Mack would fade, then be forgotten. They'd get a Christmas card from him and remember the fun they'd shared and that would be that.

In the meantime, Heather thought, curbing a smile, she most definitely would refrain from tearing Mack's clothes off his magnificent body in her mind and flinging him onto her bed.

Mack slid back into the booth, causing Heather to jerk in surprise as she was pulled from her thoughts.

"Here you go, girls," Mack said. "Tokens for the video games."

"Oh, wow," Melissa said. "We get to play video games? Cool. Thank you, Uncle Mack. Come on, Emma."

"Hold it," Heather said, raising one hand. "You

stay on this side of the rows of machines, where I can see you.''

''No-o-o-o problem,'' Emma said. ''Thank you, Uncle Mack. We never get to play video games. Take care of my Barbie doll, okay?''

''And my mitt,'' Melissa said.

''No-o-o-o problem,'' Mack said, laughing.

The girls hurried from the booth and Heather watched until she saw that they were staying where she could see them. She shifted her attention to Mack, who was frowning.

''What's wrong?'' Heather said.

''I was just thinking about the girls' reaction to finding out that I'd been shot,'' he said. ''They said they didn't want me to die like their daddy had. Do you think they need grief counseling or something, to get closure about the death of their father?''

''No, no,'' Heather said, shaking her head. ''They never even met their father.'' She paused. ''Thank goodness. Anyway, I think what happened is that they view you as a member of the family, a *male* addition. The only emotional reference they have to a man in the family is the one who died. Hence, they don't want you to die, too.''

''Oh,'' Mack said, nodding. ''You certainly know a great deal about child psychology, Heather.''

''No,'' she said, laughing, ''I was just a six-year-old girl once myself.'' She frowned. ''Besides, I have had a lot of experience projecting my past onto my present and making grave errors by doing so. I can understand the transference the girls made when they knew you had been hurt.''

''Back up, here,'' Mack said. ''You're obviously glad the girls never met their father. Was Frank one of the errors you made?''

Heather nodded. ''Mack, Frank Marshall was a selfish man, who packed up and walked out on me when I told him I was pregnant. I'm very sorry if it upsets you to learn that your brother was not what you might want to believe he was, but facts are facts.''

''Frank was my half brother,'' Mack said, ''and no, it doesn't upset me to learn he was a bum, except for it causing you such hardship and pain. Why did you marry him in the first place, if you don't mind me asking?''

''It was Basic Psychology 101,'' Heather said, shrugging. ''My seventeen-year-old unwed mother went to the store for milk and left me with my grandmother. That is the longest trip to the market in history, because she never came back.''

''Ah, man, that's rotten,'' Mack said, covering one of Heather's hands with one of his on top of the table. ''I'm so sorry.''

''It's old, old news. My grandmother was wonderful, but she passed away when I was fourteen and I was swept up into the foster care system, then out on my own when I was eighteen.

''When Frank Marshall came along, oozing charm, giving me his undivided attention, I grabbed hold and hung on. Here was my chance to belong to someone, to not be abandoned again, to be loved. I was twenty years old and I suddenly saw a future that held all my hopes and dreams.

"Oh, what a joke. Six months after Frank and I were married, I found out I was pregnant and he left. Three weeks after that, he was killed while driving drunk. End of Frank. End of story."

"Heather," Mack said, stroking the side of her hand with his thumb. "I..."

"No, please, let me finish. I'm not telling you this sordid tale to gain your sympathy—in fact, my friend Susie is the only other person I've ever confided in about my past. But I need you to understand my concerns about the girls.

"We have to remind the twins that you'll be leaving in a couple of weeks. They mustn't believe they get to keep you forever, because the fact is you won't be here with us. You...you will...be gone. And I don't want their hearts broken."

And if he didn't let go of her hand, Heather thought frantically, didn't stop that maddening, tantalizing, heat-evoking stroking with his thumb, her bones were going to dissolve.

"You're wrong, Heather," Mack said, tightening his hold on her hand. "Yes, okay, so I'll leave when I'm due to have my shoulder checked over, but I'll be back to visit in the future. The girls *will* get to keep me forever, because I'm a permanent member of the family."

"Mack, you're viewing this as an adult," Heather

said, shaking her head. "Try thinking like a six-year-old. To the twins, keeping you forever means that you never leave at all, don't you see? We can't let the girls believe that, even fantasize about it, or they'll be heartbroken when you go. I won't allow that to happen to them." She paused. "May I have my hand back, please?"

"Not yet," he said, giving her hand a gentle squeeze. "I want to tell you that I admire and respect you very much. You were dealt some lousy cards in life, but you've played out the hand with class and dignity. Melissa and Emma are extremely fortunate little girls to have you for their mother."

"Thank you," Heather said softly. "That was a lovely thing to say."

"I meant every word."

Mack looked directly into Heather's eyes as he once again began to stroke her hand with his thumb. Heather was unable to tear her gaze from Mack's, and the people, the noise, the pizza parlor itself, seemed to fade into oblivion as they were encased in a sensuous mist. It swirled around them, seeming to pull them closer and closer together even though they hadn't moved.

"Drink delivery," a voice said.

Heather and Mack jumped at the sudden intrusion, quickly pulling their hands apart to rest below the table. A teenage boy stood by their table holding a tray with a pitcher of soda and four glasses.

"Thanks," Mack said, the gritty quality of his voice echoing in his ears.

As the boy placed the pitcher and glasses on the table, Mack cleared his throat and shifted slightly in the booth, willing his aroused body back under control.

Heather Marshall, he thought, was pushing his libido buttons…big time. He'd been consumed with desire when she pinned him in place with those gorgeous dark eyes of hers.

If any other woman had looked at him the way Heather just had, he'd read that message as a "Go," and the evening would conclude with making love.

But this was Heather and he knew, just somehow knew, she didn't have a clue that desire had shown in her dark eyes, that her lips had been slightly parted, just waiting to be kissed, that there had been a flush to her cheeks caused by the same heat that had consumed him.

No, Heather wasn't like the women he knew. Not even close. Despite the fact that she'd given birth, she was an innocent, a very unworldly woman, who didn't play the game, nor know the rules.

So, he was going to have to be noble, not take advantage of Heather, even though he wanted her with an intensity that was far beyond anything he could remember experiencing before.

He'd seen the passion in Heather's eyes, but did *she* realize that she desired him? Was she even aware of what was happening between them? Surely she knew.

But then again, it had been many years since she'd been married to his half brother, and he had a feeling there had been no time, nor inclination on Heather's part, to date anyone while scrambling to provide for her daughters.

Damn, this was getting rather depressing. Heather Marshall could very well desire him as much as he did her, and not even know it. To take advantage of what he'd seen in her eyes, on her face, would put him in the same category as Frank.

"What are you scowling about?" Heather said as the waiter walked away.

"Oh...nothing," Mack said, producing a small smile. "Heather, I'm honored that you trust me enough to have told me about your past. I know you felt you had to tell me so I could better understand the twins, but...thank you." He paused. "What do the girls know about their father?"

"Very little," she said. "I've kept it simple because lies have a way of multiplying. I told the girls that their daddy was a very nice man, that I'm sorry they never had a chance to know him, and gave them a picture of him to keep in their room. Thankfully they've asked very few questions about him."

Mack nodded, then tilted his head to one side to look past her. "That's our number for the pizza. I'll be right back and I'll collect the girls when I come."

As Mack walked away, Heather sank back in the booth and placed her hand on her heart for a moment. Something strange happened when she'd looked into Mack's dark eyes, she thought. It was as though they'd been transported to another place, out of the pizza parlor, and into a mist that had virtually crackled with sensuality.

Had Mack been as suffused with raging, burning desire as she had? Did he want her the way she wanted him? Was he viewing her as a woman, not just as the mother of Emma and Melissa?

Oh, that was a silly thought. She was falling prey to Mack's masculine magnetism only because it had been so long since she'd been in close proximity to a man. Mack was probably so accustomed to being with any woman of his choice that someone with her lack of sophistication was having no effect on him whatsoever.

That was a comforting conclusion, Heather thought. It was a tad hard on the ego, but it was safe, would definitely help her to move past her overreactions to Mack and enable her to place him firmly in the role of the twins' uncle where he belonged.

And this whole scenario was becoming so confusing and complicated it was exhausting.

"I lost every game I played," Melissa said, sliding into the booth and picking up her precious mitt.

"Me, too," Emma said, sitting across from her sister. "I was blasted into bits by the evil monsters in the spaceship."

Mack placed two pizzas on the table, then settled next to Emma in the booth.

"Nothing like some violent fun games to play,"

Heather said, smiling. "That's enough of those for one night. Mmm. That pizza smells delicious."

"Dig in, ladies," Mack said. "You see before you one pizza with just cheese and one with everything on it except the little fishies." He filled the glasses with soda. "There. Is everybody happy?"

"Yep," Melissa said, reaching for a piece of the pizza with the multitude of toppings.

"Yep," Emma echoed, then took a bite of a cheese-only slice Heather had placed on her plate.

"And you, Heather?" Mack said, looking at her intently. "Are you happy?"

Mack wasn't asking her opinion about the pizza, Heather thought. He was, she somehow knew, doing a survey on her life in general. He was assuming, she supposed, that no one living how she did, where she did, could possibly be content. Well, she had news for Mr. Marshall.

"Yes," she said, lifting her chin. "I'm very happy, Mack."

Mack nodded slowly. "Mmm. You're very positive about that?"

"Very," she said.

"Oh, no," Melissa said. "I spilled soda on my new shirt."

Heather tore her gaze from Mack's, picked up a napkin, and wiped the soda from the front of Melissa's Garfield shirt.

"It won't stain, sweetie," she said. "I'll wash it in time for you to wear it to school on Monday."

"'Kay," Melissa said, then took another bite of her pizza.

That wasn't a new shirt Melissa was wearing, Mack thought, frowning. It was slightly faded and he could see a darn on one of the sleeves.

Melissa had been so excited about her *new* shirt when he'd arrived at the house, but these kids, and possibly Heather too wore secondhand clothes.

That wasn't the way it should be. They were Marshalls, part of *his* family, and they deserved better than having wardrobes of other people's castoffs. He was going to do something about it. Somehow.

"Did you think about your dream yet, Uncle Mack?" Emma said, bringing him from his thoughts. "You know, the one you don't got?"

"Don't *have,*" Heather said. "It's probably difficult to think about a missing dream when a person is on vacation, Emma. Uncle Mack will no doubt have better luck at finding his dream once he goes home to New York City. Right, Mack?"

"Oh, I don't know about that," Mack said. "I'll still be the same person, whether I'm here in Tucson or back in New York."

Heather narrowed her eyes and leaned slightly forward. "But you *are* only in Tucson for a few weeks. Right? You'll be able to think better in your own home after you *leave* here...soon." She paused. "Right, Mack?"

"Oh!" Mack nodded. "Yes. I'm on vacation. I'll need to return to work...soon."

"You can take pictures anywhere," Melissa said. "You could buy a house and live in Tucson forever if you wanted to."

"He doesn't have enough money for a house, Melissa," Emma said, "and he doesn't even have a dream piggy to save for one. Besides, Mommy said maybe Uncle Mack doesn't want a house. Do you want a house, Uncle Mack?"

"It probably wouldn't be a good idea," Mack said. "I wouldn't be there enough to mow the lawn and keep everything looking nice."

"You should quit going away all the time," Melissa said. "If you had a house, you could get a dog. That would be so cool. We're going to get a dog when we buy our dream house, aren't we, Mommy?"

"Yes, we are," Heather said. "We'll go to the pound and get a cute, *small* dog."

"Sounds good," Mack said. "When I was a boy, I really wanted a dog. I was going to name him Butch. But..." He shrugged.

"How come you never got your dog named Butch?" Melissa said.

"I lived with just my father," Mack said, "and he...well, he didn't like to stay in one place for too long. We moved to a lot of different cities while I was growing up, and it's pretty hard to have a dog when you keep packing and going."

"Oh," Melissa said. "I wouldn't like that. You had to leave your friends all the time and go to a new school and…no, that's not good at all. That's terrible, just terrible.''

"I got used to it," Mack said. "Actually, Melissa, it wasn't terrible because I still don't stay in one place for long and I've had a lot of practice at traveling because of how I grew up. Some people just don't— can't—put down roots and I'm one of them.''

"What does that mean?" Melissa said. "Put down roots? Like a tree?''

"Well, yes, sort of like a tree," Mack said, nodding. "A tree stays where it's planted, where its roots are. People do that, too, but I don't.''

"How do you know you wouldn't like to have roots like a tree," Melissa said, "if you never tried it?''

Mack opened his mouth, closed it, then chuckled. "The FBI could use this kid, Heather. She's a tough interrogator.''

"Believe me," Heather said, smiling, "I'm well aware of that. Emma is the same way. You might as well give up and answer her question. How do you know you wouldn't like to have roots like a tree if you've never tried it?''

"Well," Mack said slowly, "I've been moving around for thirty-seven years, ladies, and I believe it's rather late in the game for me to change. I'm just not capable of having roots like a tree.''

"Terrible," Melissa said. "Just terrible.''

"Don't you get sad having to say goodbye to everybody all the time?" Emma said. "I would be so-o-o sad, and lonely, and I'd cry, and cry, and cry.''

"So would I, Emma," Heather said quietly, looking at her daughter. "I wouldn't want to be living a life of goodbyes. I've had enough of those already."

"Maybe you could make having roots like a tree your very own dream, Uncle Mack," Emma said. "Then you wouldn't have to say goodbye all the time, and be sad, and lonely, and stuff."

"But I don't get sad and lonely and..." Mack started, then his voice trailed off.

A vivid image of being sprawled in the dirt, bleeding, thinking he was going to die alone in that god-forsaken place flashed in his mental vision and a chill coursed through him, causing a cold fist to tighten in his gut.

"Well, things are different now," he said, his voice slightly hoarse. "I've found all of you. I have a family. If I'm on the other side of the world and start to get lonely, I'll just think about the three of you and I'm sure I'll feel much better."

"If we're your family," Melissa said, reaching for another slice of pizza, "then you shouldn't leave us. You should stay with us forever and ever. That's what families are supposed to do." She sighed. "But they don't. Buzzy's daddy went to live with another mother, and our daddy died, and...people just don't follow the rules about families one little bit."

"Maybe that's 'cause not everybody knows what the rules are," Emma said. "We could teach you the rules about staying with us forever and ever, Uncle Mack, and then you could have roots like a tree."

"Well, I..." Mack said.

"Emma," Heather said, "Uncle Mack has said that he just isn't the kind of person who stays in one place for long. We have to respect that. Everyone is different, and just because they don't think like we do, it doesn't make them wrong. Do you understand what I'm saying?"

"No," Emma said, frowning. "Families should stay together forever and ever, and that's that."

Heather glanced heavenward. "Let's change the subject." She paused. "But you girls have got to remember that Uncle Mack will be leaving soon."

"Well, fine," Emma said, folding her arms over her chest. "But when Uncle Mack leaves, I'm going to cry. So there."

"I'll cry with you, Emma," Melissa said, nodding. "I will."

I won't, Heather thought. The only reason she would cry when Mack left would be if he was taking her heart with him. And that wasn't going to happen.

Chapter Five

Late that night Mack sat in a lounge chair on the balcony outside his hotel room, his feet propped on the metal railing. He had the small throw pillow from the sofa in the suite tucked behind his left shoulder, which was throbbing like a painful toothache. He'd taken two aspirin and was waiting for them to kick in before he even attempted to get some sleep.

Despite his physical discomfort, he was emotionally contented, filled with a sense of well-being that was rather unfamiliar but definitely welcome. And he knew the source of this new inner peace...Heather, Melissa and Emma.

Mack swept his gaze over the sky, amazed at the brilliance of the multitude of stars twinkling in the heavens. He couldn't remember when he'd stopped long enough to drink in the sight of nature's gifts such as a star-studded sky on a clear, cool spring night. He was aware of the beauty now only because Melissa and Emma had made wishes on the stars when they'd left the pizza parlor.

Heather, Melissa and Emma, he mentally repeated. His family.

Mack chuckled softly as he replayed in his head the conversation with the female Marshalls about trees and roots, and knowing the rules of being a family.

The twins pinned him to the wall when he least expected it, leaving smooth-talking Mack Marshall scrambling for a response to the questions they whipped on him.

They were really something, those little heart-stealers, so open and honest, just said whatever was on their complicated, six-year-old minds.

And Heather? Ah, yes, lovely Heather. She was as open and honest and as real as her daughters.

Mack frowned and shifted slightly on the lounge, attempting to find a comfortable position.

Heather sure had had a rough life, he mused. Really tough, and his half brother, Frank, had been a louse from the word go. But Heather wasn't bitter, or hard, didn't have an angry chip on her shoulder. She was simply…Heather, and he liked her very, very much.

Did you think about your dream yet, Uncle Mack? You know, the one you don't got?

"No, sweet Emma," Mack said out loud, then

sighed wearily. "I don't think I know how to dream anymore. The last dream I had was probably wanting that dog, ole Butch, and that never came to be."

Strange. Heather and the twins had so little materialistically, yet they were obviously happy in the world they'd created for themselves.

And they knew how to dream.

They would have their own house someday, and were working toward that dream, that goal, a penny at a time, placed in their dream piggy. There was a rainbow in their future with their very own home nestled in the pot instead of gold.

"And you, Marshall?" he said, looking up at the sky again.

He had money to burn, bought whatever he wanted when the mood struck, settled for nothing less than top-of-the-line, first-class all the way.

He was good, very good, at his chosen profession and had the awards to prove it, along with the fat checks that testified to making it to the big time.

But was he happy? No, not really. Was he *un*happy? No, not really. He just...existed, he guessed, went from one place to another doing his thing, not really dwelling on his state of mind, or taking inventory of his life.

But now, because of Heather and her daughters, he knew a glaring truth about himself.

He didn't know how to dream.

There wasn't a rainbow in *his* future, there was just more of the same and, oh, man, the years ahead seemed to be spread in front of him in a dark, cold, empty nothingness.

"Ah, hell, Marshall," he said, dragging his hands down his face. "Give it a rest."

He'd been in such an upbeat mood when he settled into the lounge out here and now he'd bummed himself out to the max. Yeah, well, he was tired, just didn't have his usual stamina back yet. And he was sick to death of being in pain. He just wanted his shoulder to heal and be done with it.

There was nothing wrong with his life, or his future. He could write his own ticket. The constant pain was wearing him down, that's all.

So what if he didn't have a damn dream? Just because two little girls had decided he needed one didn't make it an etched-in-stone thing he was sadly lacking.

The majority of people in the world probably didn't have a dream, for Pete's sake. They just…existed, plugged away one day at a time. But were they happy, those multitudes of faceless human beings? Were they happy, the way Heather and Melissa and Emma were? He doubted it. He seriously doubted it.

"Hell," Mack said, leveling himself to his feet. "I'm *definitely* depressing myself."

He picked up the throw pillow and went into the large living room of the suite, closing the sliding-glass door behind him. He narrowed his eyes as he scrutinized the area, shaking his head as he determined that the living room was nearly as large as Heather's entire dinky house.

He didn't need all this space to roam around in...alone. He'd automatically requested a suite when he'd made his hotel reservations without a second thought. Because, by damn, he was Mack Marshall and nothing but the best would do.

But hot-shot Marshall didn't know how to dream.

"Damn it," Mack said, tossing the pillow onto the sofa, "knock it off."

He started toward the bedroom, hesitated, then spun around and returned to the sofa to sit and pick up the telephone receiver. He punched in a series of numbers and drummed the fingers of his free hand on the end table as the ringing on the other end of the line began.

Four rings...five...six...

"What?" a groggy-sounding voice finally said.

"Marilyn? This is Mack."

"Mack? What's wrong?" the woman said. "Do you know what time it is?"

"Oh," Mack said. "Sorry. I didn't think about the time difference between Tucson and New York. I woke you up, didn't I?"

"Well, yes, but, hey, what's an agent for?" Marilyn said. "Do we need sleep? Of course not. We are superior beings who...why are you calling me in the middle of the night? Is your shoulder worse? You know the doctor didn't want you to make that trip yet, but would you listen? No, not Mack Marshall. You just went ahead and...are you back in the hospital out there? Talk to me."

"I would if you'd give me a chance."

"Oh. So, okay, speak."

"I just want to ask you a question, Marilyn."

"Ask away."

Mack cleared his throat. "Marilyn, do you have a dream? You know, a secret wish kind of thing? Something that you'd want to be waiting for you at the end of a rainbow? A dream?"

There was silence on the other end of the line. A very long silence.

"Marilyn?" Mack said.

"Whatever you're drinking," Marilyn said, "don't have any more. You're blitzed. Are you combining pain pills with booze, Mack? That's dangerous."

"Damn it, Marilyn, in all the years that you've been my friend and agent, have you ever known me to drink too much? No, you have not."

"Yeah, well, you've never been shot before, either. A near-death experience can change a person. Personally, I think you're drunk as a skunk. You called me in the middle of the night to ask me if I have a dream? Something I want to find at the end of a rainbow?"

"Yes. I swear to you that I'm not drunk," Mack said, his voice rising. "Would you just answer the question, for crying out loud?"

"You're serious, aren't you?" Marilyn said.

Mack hooked his free hand on the back of his neck. "Very serious."

"Well, all right, give me a minute here," Marilyn said. "A dream. A dream? I had one a long time ago, but... I wanted to be a mother, Mack. I wanted a baby.

"But then I got caught up in this crazy career and kept putting off getting involved in a serious relationship with a man, and all of a sudden it was too late and…now? No, I guess I don't have a dream anymore, not like the kind you're speaking of." She paused. "Why are we having this conversation at this god-awful hour?"

"Because it's important," Mack said. "Don't you think you need a dream to make the future mean something, to do more than just get by day after day? I mean, hell, Marilyn, where are we headed, where will we end up, people like you and me, if we don't have a dream?"

"How in the hell should I know?" she said, none too quietly. "You're the nutcase who's talking about dreams and rainbows in the middle of the night. What's with you? Who are you hanging around with out there? Oh, those long-lost relatives of yours. I take it that you found them, and they're into dreams and rainbows. Did it ever occur to you that people who live in that kind of climate have fried brains?"

"Heather, Melissa and Emma do *not* have fried brains," Mack said indignantly. "They're the most down-to-earth, real people I've ever had the privilege to meet. They're fantastic, Marilyn, they really are. What size clothes do six-year-old girls wear?"

"Huh?" Marilyn said. "You're shifting gears on me so fast I can't keep up. What about six-year-old girls?"

"Their clothes," Mack said. "All the twins have

are castoffs, used stuff. I want to buy them some new things to wear, but I don't know what size to get.''

"Is this Heather person the mother of these twins?"

"Yes."

"Well, ask *her* what size clothes her kids wear. I'd figure that six-year-olds wear size six, but what do I know about it? Nothing. Talk to Heather.''

"It's a rather touchy situation," Mack said, absently massaging his left shoulder. "I don't want to come across as if I don't approve of the way Heather provides for her children. She's doing the best she can against some tough odds and I admire her for that.''

"Tell them they won a contest and get to go on a shopping spree," Marilyn said. "How's that?"

"Ridiculous," Mack said, frowning. "I'd like to get Heather some new clothes, too, but I don't have a clue how to get her to agree to all this.''

"Any woman," Marilyn said, "who is offered a trip to a clothing store with all expenses paid is going to beat you to the door to get the show on the road.''

"Heather isn't just *any* woman," Mack said quietly. "She's different, Marilyn, very special. She's the one who taught her kids how to dream, because *she* has a dream herself. She should be bitter and angry about the way her life has gone, but she's not.

"I've never met a woman like Heather before. She's so…I don't know…so real, so honest, so…she's pretty, too. Very lovely. She has the biggest, darkest eyes I've ever seen that mirror her emotions, and long black hair that she wears in a braid, and her features are so delicate, and when she smiles her whole face lights up like sunshine and—''

''Uh-oh,'' Marilyn said. ''Me thinks the mighty has fallen.''

''What are you talking about?'' Mack said, frowning.

''Are you listening to yourself, Mack?'' Marilyn asked. ''You are very smitten...now there's a good old-fashioned word...smitten with the lovely Heather. You've got heart trouble, my boy. If I wasn't hearing this firsthand, I wouldn't believe it had happened. Mack Marshall is down for the count.''

''You're crazy, Marilyn,'' Mack said. ''Your brain obviously doesn't function on all cylinders in the middle of the night. I like Heather very much, as a person, a woman, and respect her for what she has accomplished. But I don't have heart trouble, as you so quaintly put it, over her. She's not even my type. Not even close. I mean, well, sure, I'm attracted to her, and she kicks my libido into overdrive at times, but that doesn't mean anything on an emotional level.''

Marilyn laughed. ''Yeah, right. Oh, this is a hoot. I can see the story now that will be in the newspaper. 'World-famous photojournalist, Mack Marshall, who was voted one of New York City's top five eligible bachelors last year, has married a lovely lass named Heather and become the instant father of six-year-old twin girls.' Ta-da. We'll hear the wailing of women all across the country.''

Mack rolled his eyes heavenward. "Go back to sleep, Marilyn. You need your rest."

"What *you* need is a reality check, buster," Marilyn said. "You've definitely got heart trouble. Hey, I think it's great, I really do. I'm happy for you, Mack. I say go for it. It might mean you won't be traveling to the hot spots around the globe like you always have, but I've got a publisher who is panting for another book from you. You can settle in with your wife and kiddies and put together another bestseller, from which I'll take my percentage and go on a cruise."

"Good night, Marilyn," Mack said, shaking his head.

"Okay, dust me off, but time will prove me right. I'm serious about you doing another book, Mack. Your publisher called me again. They are offering very big bucks, and I haven't even begun my tough negotiating number. Think about it, will you?"

"Yeah, okay, I'll think about it."

"As for Heather and the cutie-pies?" Marilyn said. "You'd better pay attention, because the writing is on the wall. 'Bye for now and good luck with the dream and rainbow bit, and if you decide to call me again, figure out what time it is here first, would you?"

"Yes, I will. Sorry I woke you. 'Bye, Marilyn," Mack said, then replaced the receiver.

He stared at the telephone, a deep frown on his face.

Heart trouble? his mind echoed. As in, losing his heart, falling in love with Heather Marshall? Marilyn was way out in left field on that one.

He didn't have *heart* trouble in regard to Heather, he had...*body* trouble. He desired her with an intensity that was far beyond the norm. For some unknown reason, Heather was capable of pushing his sensual buttons as no woman he'd ever known before.

Granted, something very strange had happened at the pizza parlor when Heather gazed at him with those incredible eyes of hers. She was a spell-weaver, had caused him to feel as though he'd been transported to a sensuous place where only the two of them were allowed to go. That had been unsettling. But Marilyn had read what he said all wrong.

Yeah, well, what did he expect when he woke a person up from a dead sleep in the middle of the night? Her brain had been foggy, that was for sure.

Calling his agent in the first place had been a dumb thing to do, now that he really thought about it. "Hi, Marilyn, do you have a dream?" Cripe, no wonder she figured he was drunk.

"Go to bed," Mack said, getting to his feet to head for the bedroom. "Get some sleep, Marshall, before you do some other fool thing."

A short time later, Mack shifted on the mattress to find a comfortable place for his aching shoulder, and willed himself to ignore the nagging pain.

Damn, he thought. He had a whole day to fill tomorrow, wouldn't see Heather and the twins until the evening when he arrived at their door with the takeout Chinese food he'd said he would like to bring.

The girls were spending the morning down the

street with someone they called Grandma Hill, so that Heather could work on income tax returns. This was her busiest season, she'd explained, and she put in long hours. In the afternoon, the twins were going to a birthday party and Heather would keep plugging away on the computer.

She worked so damn hard, Mack mused as sleep began to creep over his senses. And for what? So she could live in a place the size of a postage stamp and buy her kids used clothes?

No, it was more than that. Heather knocked herself out so there would be pennies to put in the piggy. She scrambled for every dime because Heather Marshall had a dream.

And that seemed to make all the difference in the world.

Heather placed the large envelope on top of two others, then gave the stack a satisfied pat. She leaned back in the chair where she was sitting in front of the computer and stretched her arms above her head, rotating her neck at the same time.

She'd completed three tax returns today, she thought, allowing her hands to fall into her lap. The work had just zoomed along with no problems, no glitches, no questions she had to telephone the clients about.

She'd been aware through the hours she'd spent at the computer that she was in an upbeat mood, had even found herself humming a peppy tune at times.

Heather frowned, got to her feet, then crossed the short distance to the bed and sank onto the edge.

She knew *why* she'd felt so light-hearted all day, she thought, staring into space. There was no sense denying it; she'd only be running from the truth if she did. She'd been a happy camper since waking that morning because she was looking forward to the evening, and the arrival of Mack Marshall.

Well, that was understandable. Wasn't it? Sure. Mack was nice to be with, and it was fun watching and listening as he interacted with the girls. He very often got caught off guard by her little chatterboxes.

Nice try, Heather, she told herself. There was more to her sense of anticipation about the coming evening than just witnessing Mack with the twins. She herself wanted to be with Mack, to hear his laughter, to see his smile, to bask in the wondrous sense of her own womanliness that he evoked whenever she was with him.

"Oh, dear," she said, pressing her hands to her cheeks that felt suddenly warm and flushed. "This is *not* good."

Well, is wasn't *bad*, either, really. She'd figured out why she continually overreacted to Mack. And her conclusions were sound. It wasn't Mack himself who caused her heart to race and heated desire to swirl within her. It was simply a matter of...supply and demand. There had been no *supply* of men since the twins had been born, and her body was *demanding* to explore her femininity, which had been in cold storage for years.

But...

It was Mack Marshall who caused her to feel so special. It was Mack whom she desired, wished to make love with, although that would never happen. It was Mack's laughter she wanted to hear, his smile she wanted to see, his aroma she wanted to inhale and savor.

No, now stop it. She'd feel this way about any man who had appeared out of nowhere and spent so much time with her and Melissa and Emma.

Wouldn't she?

"Quit thinking, Heather," she said out loud as she got to her feet.

She had this all analyzed and was comfortable with her conclusions. She'd just confuse herself if she started questioning her own logic. Enough of this.

But why had she mentally changed her plans four times about what she would wear tonight to eat Chinese food in her own kitchen? Why had she quit work early enough to be able to wash her hair so it would look its best? Why was she counting down the minutes until Mack would arrive at the house?

Oh, darn it, why was she asking herself these frightening questions? She was going to grab hold of her supply-and-demand theory and hang on to it for dear life before she scared herself to death.

"Got it," she said with a decisive nod.

The twins were watching television when Heather

entered the living room, the contents from the goodie bags they'd received at the birthday party they'd attended spread out in front of them.

"I'm going to take a shower and wash my hair, my sweets," Heather said. "Don't eat any more of that candy you got because Uncle Mack is bringing us Chinese food for dinner."

"Do I like Chinese food?" Melissa said.

Heather laughed. "I have no idea. You've never had it before." She paused. "Answer the telephone if it rings while I'm in the shower, please, and take a message if necessary."

"'Kay," Melissa said. "I sure hope I like Chinese food."

"I'll like it," Emma said.

"How do you know you will?" Melissa said. "If I've never had any, then you've never had any."

"I'll like it because Uncle Mack is bringing it," Emma said. "He wouldn't ask us to eat something that is yucky, Melissa. Uncle Mack just wouldn't do that."

"Oh…yeah," Melissa said slowly. "You're right. 'Kay, I'll like Chinese food just fine, too."

"There is definitely hero worship taking place in this house," Heather said.

"There's what?" Melissa said.

"Never mind," Heather said, spinning around. "I'm going to wash my hair."

Half an hour later Heather emerged from the bathroom in the hallway wearing black slacks and a black-

and-gray striped top. She'd blown her hair dry and it tumbled in waves to the middle of her back. She'd broken the rubber band from the end of her braid when she'd undone it, and was heading down the hall toward the kitchen and the box of rubber bands that were in a drawer.

When she entered the living room, she stopped so suddenly she teetered for a moment.

"Mack," she said, then glanced quickly at her watch. "I didn't expect...you're early."

Mack got to his feet, his gaze riveted on Heather.

"I know I am," he said. "I hit it lucky at the Chinese restaurant and didn't have to wait long to... Your hair is beautiful, Heather. I wondered what it would look like if you allowed it to fall free instead of braiding it and...an ebony waterfall. Sensational."

"Thank you," Heather said softly, hardly able to breathe. "I was on my way to get a rubber band for the end of my braid because I broke the one that—"

"No, please," Mack said, raising one hand. "Don't braid it tonight. Leave it just as it is. Please?"

"Yes, all right," she said, then took a much-needed breath.

Beautiful? she thought incredulously. Her hair was beautiful and sensational? An ebony waterfall? *Her* hair? She never gave two seconds thought to it. It was just hair. Beautiful? Well, gracious, fancy that.

"Well," she said, hoping her voice was steadier than it sounded as it echoed in her ears, "are we ready to eat Chinese food?"

"We'll like it," Emma said to Mack.

"Yep, we will," Melissa said. "We've never had Chinese food before but we'll like it just fine."

"You've never eaten Chinese food?" Mack said, looking at one twin, then the other. "That's amazing. Well, good. Great. This will be a first for you then. An experience you've never had before. I, um, I had a brand-new experience myself today."

"What was it?" Melissa said.

"Heather," Mack said, "we can heat the food in your microwave in a bit, if that's all right with you. I'd like to share my new experience with all of you first."

"Certainly," Heather said, sitting in the rocking chair.

If there was ever a time for some smooth talking, this was it, Mack thought as he sat down on the sofa between the twins. He had to present this right, because he was liable to find himself sent packing if he blew it.

But how in the hell was he supposed to concentrate on what he was about to say when he was consumed with pulsing, heated desire for Heather Marshall? Her hair. That glorious hair had knocked him for a loop. Oh, man, he wanted to sink his fingers into it, pull it forward, watch it slide like dark, silken threads over Heather's bare breasts and—

"Uncle Mack?" Melissa said.

"What!" he said much too loudly. "Sorry. Didn't mean to yell. My mind wandered for a minute there."

"No-o-o-o problem," Emma said. "That happens to old people. Grandma Hill says her mind goes for a walk around the block without her sometimes and she has to wait until it gets back so she can remember what she was going to say."

Mack chuckled. "Well, as a member of the old people set, I appreciate your patience and understanding." He cleared his throat. "Now, then, where was I? Oh, yes, I was going to share my new experience with you."

"Yep," Melissa said.

"Well, you see," Mack said, feeling a trickle of sweat slither down his back, "I'd never had a conversation with any little girls, or boys, either, for that matter, until I met you two. Just getting to know you has been a new experience and I'm enjoying every minute of it."

"Oh," Melissa said.

"So," Mack went on, sliding a quick glance at Heather who was listening intently to what he was saying, "I decided to have another new experience in regard to you ladies."

"What was it?" Melissa said.

"I went shopping for clothes for you, because I've never had a chance to do that before. If it wasn't for you, I never would have known how much fun it is to pick out things for special little girls. I really appreciate the fact that…well, that you're here."

"You bought…" Heather said, getting to her feet.

"Mack, I wish you would have discussed this with me beforehand."

"To make certain that I purchased the right sizes?" he said, an expression of pure innocence on his face. "Well, I described everyone to the saleswoman and she helped me select things, but I have the receipts in case anything needs to be exchanged. I sure enjoyed myself and, like I said, I thank all of you for being my family."

Heather threw up her hands in defeat and sank back onto the rocker. "I'm glad we could make it possible for you to have such a pleasurable new experience. I mean, hey, what are families for?"

"Are you mad about something, Mommy?" Emma said. "Your lips are skinny like they get when you're mad."

"No, sweetheart," Heather said, producing a small smile, "I'm not angry. I'm just used to making all the decisions regarding you girls, and new clothes from a mall are not what we...never mind."

"Then it's all right?" Mack said. "I can bring in the clothes? I left them in my vehicle out front until I determined if this was acceptable to you, Heather."

"A question," she said, looking at him pointedly, "that should have been asked before you *shared* your new experience with us."

"But there's no such thing as having too many clothes, is there?" Mack said, raising his eyebrows. "I've heard women say that. You can never have too many clothes. Yes, sir, they say that all the time, so I figured I couldn't be off base here. Right? Anyway, it was a terrific new experience and again I say thank-you to you all.'' He got to his feet. ''Come on, girls, you can help me with the shopping bags.''

As the trio left the house, with the excited twins running ahead of Mack, Heather leaned her head back against the rocker and sighed.

She was going to strangle that man, she thought. He had no right to buy her daughters new clothes. New. From a mall. With price tags she just knew would make her cringe.

She and the twins wore used clothing that was per-fectly adequate and...how dare that Mack Marshall be so pushy, so overbearing, so...thoughtful and dear, and willing to spend his leisure hours doing something for her daughters that had no doubt made him feel inadequate. But he had been willing to ask a sales-woman to help him, to put his male pride aside to accomplish his goal.

How dare he? He dared because he viewed himself as Melissa's and Emma's uncle, a member of the fam-ily, someone who could afford to buy new clothes so he went out and bought them. He dared because he cared.

If she refused to allow the girls to accept these gifts, she'd be eligible for the Mean Mother of the Year Award.

Oh, heavens, her life was becoming so complicated, so confusing. Everything was changing so fast.

For the first time in their lives, her daughters were

going to have brand-new clothes to wear to school. She was happy for them, she was, but it wasn't their reality. The next time they needed something to wear, they'd be back at the used-clothing store, looking for things that weren't too stained, too faded, too stretched out of shape.

Mack Marshall was changing their world, and the cold knot in her stomach said this was wrong, very wrong.

Because Mack was going to leave soon.

He was going to leave and take this fairy tale with him.

Chapter Six

It was Christmas in March.

Despite her misgivings about Mack's expensive shopping spree, Heather was soon caught up in the excitement, unable to keep from smiling as she watched Emma and Melissa nearly burst with joy over their treasures.

Melissa received four pairs of jeans in bright colors—blue, red, green and yellow—each having a coordinating top. There was also a baseball shirt with the name Marshall across the back in heat-pressed letters.

When Melissa hugged the baseball shirt tightly, Heather had to blink away tears as she saw the rapture on her daughter's face.

For Emma there were four dresses. One was a bouquet of pastel flowers, another was pale pink with lace on the collar and the edges of the short, puffy sleeves, a white one had a border-print of tumbling, prancing and sleeping kittens, and a sunny yellow creation had a satin sash around the waist. With each dress was a pair of matching socks with lace on the cuffs.

Mack had brought his camera and moved around the room, taking pictures as the twins revealed the wonders in the shiny silver shopping bags.

Sitting in the rocking chair, Heather shifted her gaze from the girls to Mack as he hunkered down to snap more pictures. Her heart fluttered as she saw the material of his slacks pull taut against his muscled thighs and his shirt stretch across his broad shoulders.

Mack moved with ease and masculine grace; he was obviously a man who was very comfortable in his own body. And *her* body was going nuts just watching him doing what had gained him world-wide recognition.

Heather frowned.

The last time he'd used that camera with the intensity she was now witnessing, Mack had been shot and nearly died in a country on the far side of the globe.

A chill swept through her as she envisioned Mack bleeding, lying on the ground, each second that help didn't arrive bringing him closer to death. No! Dear heaven, she couldn't bear the thought of anything happening to Mack. He had become very important to her very quickly, and was an intricate part of her life.

Calm down, she ordered herself. Back up. Get this right. Mack had become very important to her *and* the twins. He was the uncle, part of the family. No one with any compassionate feelings would want harm to come to a member of their family. Her fears for Mack's safety weren't borne of a woman worried about her man, but of her concern for a member of the family. Okay. She had that straight now.

"Mommy," Melissa said, "will you wash our new clothes so we can wear the one we pick to school on Monday? Please, Mom?"

"Honey," Heather said, "you don't have to wash clothes from the mall before you wear them."

"Oh," Melissa said. "I didn't know that."

"That's because," Heather said, then sighed, "because you've never had clothes from a mall before. This is a very special event and...and it won't happen again, so it's time for you girls to thank your uncle Mack for your wonderful presents."

Mack was bending over, still taking pictures when the girls flung themselves at him, nearly causing him to topple backward. Heather's breath caught as she saw Mack wince with pain as the twins hugged him tightly, chorusing their thank-yous over and over.

"You're very welcome," Mack said, managing to stand erect. "Remember, if something doesn't fit, we can take it back and exchange it."

"Can we try on our stuff, Mom?" Melissa asked.

"We'll have a fashion show," Emma said. "A real fashion show."

"That will be fun," Heather said, smiling at them.

"But let's eat dinner first, then have the fashion show."

"Wait," Mack said. "There's one more shopping bag to open."

He retrieved the glittering bag from the side of the sofa, then crossed the room and handed it to Heather.

"This one is for you," he said. "I hope you like it and I hope it fits, but...hey, it can go back for something else if...what I mean is...well, look at me...I'm a nervous wreck. I've never bought a dress for a woman before in my life. Open it, Heather, before I turn into a complete blithering idiot."

"Open it, Mommy," Melissa said, jumping up and down. "Hurry."

"But..." Heather started, then shook her head. "I can't accept a..."

"Heather, please," Mack said quietly. "Let me have this moment, these memories. Going shopping like I did, buying these things, was a totally new experience for me and it was really special. Just enjoy your gift. Please?"

Heather met Mack's gaze for a long moment, then nodded slowly.

"Yes, all right," she said softly. "Thank you. Thank you very much."

"Open it, Mom," Emma said, hopping from one foot to the other.

Heather removed the tissue from the top of the large bag, then reached in and grasped material that felt butter-soft in her hand. She stood, the bag falling to the floor as she revealed a dress that was the color of a sun-kissed peach.

Tears filled her eyes as she held the dress against her shoulders, the skirt floating in soft folds below her knees, the lacy, camisole top blousing at her waist.

"Oh-h-h," Emma said, awe ringing in her voice. "That is so beautiful. It's a dress for a princess."

"Wow," Melissa said. "You *will* look like a princess in that dress, Mom." She paused and frowned. "But you don't go anywhere that princesses go."

"There's a thought," Mack said. "You're right, Melissa. Well, I'll just have to fix that. How's this? I'll hire a baby-sitter for you and Emma one night, then take your mother out to dinner to a really fancy restaurant where princesses go to eat."

"Perfect," Emma said, clasping her hands beneath her chin.

"That's cool," Melissa said, nodding her approval.

"Heather?" Mack said. "How does that plan sound to you?"

Heather raised her head, tears still shimmering in her eyes, and smiled at Mack.

"Hold it right there," Mack said, then lifted the camera and snapped off three quick pictures in a row. "Now then, Princess Heather, would you do me the honor of dining with me very soon in a place fit for the princess that you will be in that dress?"

"Yes," Heather whispered. "I...I don't know what to say, Mack. This is the most gorgeous dress I've ever had. Thank you doesn't seem like enough to express..."

Mack stepped forward and dropped a quick kiss on Heather's lips.

"You're welcome," he said. "Okay, troops, into the kitchen. We've got Chinese food to eat and I'm a starving man."

The girls ran out of the living room, headed toward the kitchen. Mack set his camera on the rocking chair, then moved close to Heather again and framed her face in his hands.

"That little peck was to say you're welcome for the dress," he said, his voice slightly raspy. "This one is to say that I need to kiss you, Heather. I truly do—" he lowered his head toward hers "—need to kiss you."

Mack's mouth melted over Heather's in a kiss that was tender and soft and so tantalizing that she dropped the dress, creating a peach-colored pool at their feet.

She wrapped her arms around Mack's waist and as the kiss intensified, her lashes drifted down as she savored the taste, the feel, the ecstasy of the kiss they were sharing.

Mack parted Heather's lips and delved his tongue into her mouth, finding her tongue, stroking it.

He'd waited an eternity for this kiss, he thought hazily. But, oh, man, it had been worth the agonizing wait. Heather was returning his kiss in total abandon, holding nothing back. He was going up in flames of desire, wanting this incredible woman, needing her to quell the fire burning out of control within him.

"When you're done thanking Uncle Mack for the princess dress, Mom," Melissa said, "can we eat the Chinese food stuff?"

Heather and Mack jerked apart, and Mack took a step backward. Heather reached down for the forgotten dress, lifted it, dropped it, then grabbed it off the floor. Mack looked at Melissa over his shoulder as he willed his aroused body back under his control.

"Get some napkins," he said, his voice sounding hoarse to his own ears. "And forks. I don't think you guys are ready for chopsticks."

"'Kay," Melissa said, then spun around and ran out of the room again.

"Heather," Mack said.

"No," she said, spreading the dress over the top of the rocking chair, then sucking in a trembling breath. "Don't say anything. That shouldn't have happened and I don't wish to discuss it."

"Heather, look at me."

"The girls are waiting, Mack."

"Look...at...me."

Heather turned to meet Mack's gaze. Crossing her arms and wrapping her hands around her elbows, she lifted her chin.

"What happened—that kiss—wasn't wrong," he said. "It was very, very right. You kissed me back, Heather, gave as much as you took, shared equally in that kiss. You can't deny that."

''No, I can't,'' she said, ''but I'm not going where that kiss was leading to.'' She shook her head. ''No.''

''Why not? What are you afraid of?''

''Oh, Mack, for heaven's sake,'' she said, throwing up her hands. ''I'm not one of your sophisticated New York City women. I don't have casual flings, quicky affairs, then bid my lover goodbye without a second thought. That's the key word here, Mack. Goodbye. You'll be leaving soon, remember? I am not, *am not,* going to bed with you and run the risk of...'' She stopped speaking and sighed. ''No.''

''Risk of falling in love with me?'' he said. ''Hey, it works both ways, you know. What if I fell in love with you, then had to shuffle off to my life in New York?''

''Give me a break,'' she said, planting her hands on her hips. ''You've had a great deal of experience in having affairs then saying goodbye.''

''Okay, score one point for you,'' he said. ''However, there's a major difference here, Ms. Marshall.''

''Do tell,'' she said, narrowing her eyes.

Mack dragged one thumb over Heather's lips and she shivered from the sensuous foray.

''I have never in my entire life,'' he said, his voice very low and rumbly, ''desired a woman the way I do you. You're frightened about what emotions might come into play here? Well, let me tell you, lady, you scare the hell out of me. But I want you, Heather, every bit as much as you want me. Risks? Yeah, they're there...big time. But having you, making love with you, would be worth every risk taken, because when I leave, no one could ever erase the memories I'd have of what we'd shared together.'' He paused. ''Think about it.''

Mack turned and strode toward the kitchen. Heather closed her eyes for a long moment to regain her composure, then walked slowly across the living room.

Think about it? she thought. Think about what it would be like to make love with Mack Marshall? To be the recipient of all that masculine power and intensity? Think about the memories there would be of that incredible joining, memories that would be hers to keep forever?

Think about it? The problem now was to figure out how *not* to think about it. Oh, dear heaven, she was teetering on the edge of a dangerous abyss, actually leaning toward flinging herself into a place where heartache might very well be waiting to stake its claim on her.

No, no, no, she must *not* succumb to the raging desire that Mack evoked in her. No.

''Are you listening to yourself, Heather Marshall?'' she whispered.

She took a weary breath, produced a smile and entered the kitchen.

The Chinese food was consumed with the twins declaring that they liked it ''just fine.'' The conversation was lively and fun, with Mack pronouncing the name of each exotic dish in the little white boxes, and the girls attempting to say them in return, which resulted in fits of laughter.

After the kitchen was cleaned, the fashion show took place. One by one the girls put on their new outfits in their bedroom, then zoomed back into the living room to twirl around and bow to the applause from Heather and Mack.

And there, always there, was the nearly palpable sensuality crackling through the air between Heather and Mack, weaving around them, causing them to be so incredibly *aware* of the other.

Everything Mack had purchased fit perfectly, and Melissa and Emma were thrilled. Mack took a multitude of pictures during the performance. When the fashion show ended, Heather instructed the excited twins to put on their nighties.

"'Kay," Melissa said, "but aren't you going to try on your princess dress, Mom?"

"Not tonight," Heather said.

"Why not?" Emma said. "We showed you how we looked in all our beautiful clothes. I want to see you in your princess dress."

Heather smiled. "I'll model it for you the night I go to the restaurant where princesses eat." Please accept that explanation, sweethearts. She wasn't about to announce that she didn't own a strapless bra that the lacy top of the dress would require, and that she didn't have a pair of shoes fancy enough to wear with the gorgeous creation. "Okay? That will be more fun."

"'Kay," Emma said. "But how will you know that it will fit?"

"Because I saw the tag and it's exactly my size," Heather said. "Okay, it's bedtime. Bring your new clothes back out here and I'll help you hang them up in the closet in the morning. Run along now and brush your teeth and get your nighties on."

"Will you tuck us in and hear our prayers, Uncle Mack?" Emma said.

"I'd be honored to," Mack said, nodding.

"Cool," Melissa said, then she and Emma ran from the room.

They returned with their new clothes, which they laid carefully on the end of the sofa, then dashed off again.

"Goodness," Heather said. She didn't look at Mack where he sat on the sofa as she set the rocking chair in motion. "I hope they can calm down and go to sleep. They're so happy, so excited, and I thank you again for your generous and thoughtful gifts."

"It was my pleasure, believe me," Mack said. "This was really a great evening." He paused. "I'll remember *everything* that happened here tonight."

Heather's head snapped around and she looked at Mack, but before she could speak, the twins returned, clad in matching pink cotton nightgowns.

"That was quick," Heather said, getting to her feet. "Are you sure those teeth got a good brushing?"

"Yep," Melissa said, then opened her mouth wide to show her mother.

"Dazzling," Heather said. "Okay, let's go."

"Come on, Uncle Mack," Emma said, taking one of his hands.

In the small bedroom Mack glanced quickly around, frowning as he saw the cramped quarters the girls shared. There were twin beds, each set against a wall; a battered dresser between them. Mack's jaw tightened when he saw a framed photograph, on top of the dresser.

No, he wasn't going to comment on the fact that that must be a picture of his half brother, Frank, the twins' father, the man who had caused such hardship and heartbreak in Heather's life. Frank didn't deserve to have his name mentioned during this night that belonged to Heather, Melissa, Emma and Mack.

He continued his perusal of the room and saw the meager remaining space along the wall that contained toys and books on narrow shelves constructed of cinder blocks and boards that had been painted with white enamel. On the center of the top shelf was a pale pink piggy bank about the size of a football.

"This must be the dream piggy," Mack said, giving it a friendly pat.

"Yep," Melissa said. "That's it."

"You need to get a—" Emma started.

"Oh, no, you don't," Heather said. "Don't start with the business of how Uncle Mack needs a dream, Emma. It's bedtime. Prayers, please, ladies."

The girls got into bed, laid down, then folded their hands.

"God bless Mommy," they said in unison, "and my sister, and all the people I love. Amen."

"That means Uncle Mack too, please, God," Emma said. "Amen, again."

A sudden tightness gripped Mack's throat. These little girls sure knew how to throw a powerful emotional punch.

"Thank you," he said, then cleared his throat.

Blankets were straightened by Heather and Mack, hugs and kisses were exchanged, then the light was turned out.

"Good night," Heather said. "I love you to pieces. See you in the morning."

"'Night," Melissa said.

"'Night," Emma echoed. "Love you."

Back in the living room, Heather began to straighten the new clothes, mumbling something about not wanting to have to iron everything before the girls could wear them. Mack settled back onto his spot on the end of the sofa and watched her, not speaking.

"There," Heather said finally. "That's better."

"Are you finished avoiding looking at me?" Mack said quietly. "You don't have to be afraid of me, Heather. I'm not going to pounce on you."

Heather sighed, then crossed the room to sit in the rocking chair.

"I know that," she said, meeting Mack's gaze. "You wouldn't attempt to...to take anything from me that I wasn't willing to give. Would you, Mack?"

"No, I wouldn't, and I'm relieved that you realize that."

"Yes, I do," she said, "but it puts a tremendous burden on me. I can come to you right now, make it clear that I want you to kiss me, or I can tell you never to touch me again while you're visiting us."

Mack nodded. "That's true. It's up to you. I know where I stand on the issue, but I'm not going to pressure you in any way. I'm sorry that you feel uncomfortable, burdened, as you say, by…this. Believe me, that wasn't my intention. I was just being completely honest with you and…" He paused. "I think that's enough said on the subject for now. When would you like to go out to dinner in your princess dress?"

"You really don't have to do that," she said.

"I want to. Don't you?"

"Well, I…yes, of course, I do," Heather said. "It has been years since I've gone out to a fancy restaurant in a pretty dress. In fact, if I've ever done that, I don't remember. I'll feel like Cinderella for a night."

"Good." Mack nodded. "When?"

"There's a teenage girl on the street who baby-sits," Heather said, "but it shouldn't be on a school night because I'd really be like Cinderella, watching the clock to be certain I didn't get back too late for her bedtime."

"Fair enough," Mack said. "Why don't you see if she's free Friday night? I'll pay her whatever she charges. Let me know when it's set so I can make a reservation at a restaurant fit for a princess."

Heather leaned her head back on the high top of the rocker and stared at the ceiling.

"A princess," she said softly. "And Cinderella. Fairy-tale characters. That's who I'll be on that night. A make-believe person, someone I'm pretending to be in my beautiful dress, dining at an exclusive restaurant in the company of a handsome man."

"There's nothing wrong with that, Heather."

She lifted her head again and looked at him. "No, there isn't, as long as I don't forget who I really am during those hours."

"I doubt seriously that Cinderella was thinking about the hearth she had to clean at home while she was dancing with the prince at the ball," Mack said. "And why should she? It was her night. Her memories to keep."

"Well, yes, that's true."

"Do you think you could do that when we go out?" Mack said. "Just be Cinderella at the ball? No hearths to clean, no income tax returns to prepare, no household budget to worry about?"

Heather smiled. "That sounds heavenly. A few hours with no responsibilities, nothing on my mind except having a lovely time."

"There you go," Mack said, matching her smile. "Can you do it?"

"I'm certainly going to give it my best shot," she said, laughing. "I'd be crazy not to."

"Good." Mack got to his feet. "I'd better be on my way. Where did my camera end up?"

Heather stood. "I think it's under all those pretty clothes on the sofa."

Mack retrieved his camera and went to the door with Heather following behind him.

"May I see you tomorrow?" he said, turning to look at her.

"I have to work all day," Heather said. "The girls will be with Buzzy and his mother, Susie. It's not my idea of a relaxing Sunday, but at this time of year I have no choice but to glue myself to my computer every spare minute I can find."

Mack nodded. "I see."

"Why don't you come for dinner on Monday? Are you in the mood for a home-cooked meal?"

"Sold," Mack said, smiling.

"Five o'clock?" Heather said. "The girls are used to eating early."

"I'll be here." Mack paused. "Well, it was a great evening. I really enjoyed it. Every minute."

"Thank you again for the..."

"Shh," he said, placing one fingertip gently on her lips. "No more thank-yous. Let's just say that a good time was had by all, and leave it at that."

"All right."

"So, good night, Heather."

"Yes. Good night, Mack." Heather sighed. "Oh, I'm such a muddled mess. Part of me says I should shoo you out that door, and another part wants you to kiss me before you go. I could stand here for twenty minutes and probably not be able to reach a decision because it's all so new, so confusing.''

"How about a compromise?" Mack hung the strap to the camera on the doorknob, then took a step forward and cradled Heather's face in his hands. "We'll share a...a quick, little kiss. A short, good-night type of kiss. There. How's that?"

"That sounds like a feasible solution to my dilemma," Heather said softly.

Mack looked directly into Heather's eyes for a long, heart-stopping moment, then lowered his head and claimed her lips with his own.

The kiss was an explosion of senses, of heat that rocketed throughout them instantly. Heather encircled Mack's neck with her arms, being careful to not bump his left shoulder as she nestled against him, savoring his taste and aroma, the steely strength of his body.

Mack raised his head a fraction of an inch to take a rough breath, then slanted his mouth in the opposite direction, capturing Heather's lips once again.

The kiss went on and on, and desires soared to a fever pitch of want and need.

Enough, Marshall, Mack's mind whispered, then increased in volume. He was losing his grip on control, was running the risk of frightening Heather, of pushing her into a place where she might very well tell him to never touch her again. He had to stop kissing her now. *Right now.*

Mack broke the kiss and gripped Heather's shoulders, easing her slowly away from his aroused body.

She blinked, as though coming out of a trance, then stepped back and clasped her hands in front of her.

"So much for compromise," she said, then took a shuddering breath. "That was definitely *not* a quick, little kiss."

Mack dragged a hand through his hair. "I'm sorry. I..."

"Oh, no, Mack, don't apologize," she said. "I wasn't exactly beating you off with a stick. I was an equal partner in...no, I'm not going to talk it to death. I'm just going to say good night now."

"Good night, Heather," Mack said. He retrieved his camera and opened the door. "I'll see you Monday night. Five o'clock sharp."

Heather nodded, then Mack left the house, closing the door behind him with a click. Outside he stopped with his back to the door, then stiffened as he heard the lock being snapped into place, the sound seeming to be magnified tenfold.

Locked out, he thought, starting forward slowly. Locked out of that shabby little house that was filled to overflowing with warmth and laughter. Locked out, until the next time he was allowed to enter and bask in what was within those walls.

Locked out of Heather's heart, as well?

When Mack reached his vehicle that was parked at the curb, he turned and looked back at the house just as the lights went out inside.

A chill swept through him and he frowned in self-disgust. Locked out of Heather's heart? he mentally repeated. Man, that was corny. He didn't want the key to Heather Marshall's heart, for cripe's sake. He didn't want her to fall in love with him any more than he intended to fall in love with her. That would lead to guaranteed heartbreak when he left Tucson.

No, love—falling in love—wasn't part of his plan. Not even close. He desired Heather more than any woman he'd ever known. And she desired him, too. He knew she did.

Sure, making love was risky. But they were aware of those risks now, would each hold fast to the keys to their hearts, and not allow the other to take possession.

No one would get hurt.

Chapter Seven

The next day Mack was able to find a photography shop that was open and willing to rent him darkroom time. He developed the pictures he'd taken the previous night at Heather's, smiling as he clipped the wet photos on the line strung across the small room.

Melissa and Emma, he thought, looking at the prints, were definitely happy little girls. He'd captured the pure joy on their faces as they saw each new article of clothing that he had bought them. The picture of Melissa hugging her baseball shirt was fantastic, would tug at the heart of anyone who saw it.

Mack switched his attention to the developing tray and his heart began to thunder as the photograph came slowly into view. It was Heather. Heather holding the princess dress. Heather with tears shimmering in her eyes and a soft smile on her face.

Look at her, Mack thought as he clipped the picture on the line. She was so beautiful, the emotions radiating from her lovely face so real and honest.

He had caused Heather to have that expression. *He* had caused her dark eyes to glisten with tears of wonder and awe over the dress that was fit for a princess to wear. *He* had made Heather happy, and he felt about ten feet tall.

Still staring at the photograph, Mack allowed the memories of holding and kissing Heather to fill his mind. He felt the heat of desire begin to coil deep within him and welcomed it, wanted to relive every moment of what he had shared with Heather Marshall.

This was what it would be like when he left Tucson, he thought suddenly, a frown replacing his smile. He'd replay memories of Heather in his mind, would look at her photograph, attempt to recall the exact sound of her laughter, the sweet taste of her lips as he kissed her, her aroma of soap and flower-scented shampoo.

That was all he would have…memories.

Damn it, he knew that, had in fact made a sincere attempt to convince Heather that the memories they would each possess would be enough, would be worth taking the risk.

So why was he suddenly feeling so chillingly stark and empty, and very, very lonely, as he envisioned the future? Hell, he didn't know, but he'd better figure it out fast, because this dark mood was unsettling, to say the least.

Mack frowned as he began to clean up from the processing of his film.

In the past, he mused, whenever he was developing his photographs, his entire focus was on what he had captured on film. Even when he'd processed the rolls of film from the time he'd been shot, he hadn't dwelled on what had happened to him, he had centered his attention on what he was seeing, what pictures might have potential to be published.

But today? The pictures of Heather and the twins had brought the trio right into that small room with him as though they were actually standing there watching him.

Why? He didn't know. Did it make sense? No. Was it driving him nuts? Definitely.

"Get a grip, Marshall," he said out loud. "Think it through."

Okay, wait. A thought was forming in his mind. Yes, there it was. Sure. The reason he'd felt the nearly tangible presence of Heather and the girls in the dark room was that, unlike the people in the thousands of pictures he'd taken over the years, he *knew* Heather and the twins. They were more than just faces in a photograph; they were living, breathing human beings whom he interacted with beyond the lens of his camera.

"Bingo," Mack said, nodding decisively. "That's it. I'm not crazy, after all."

He began to slide the now-dry photographs into individual clear-plastic page covers, which he placed in a leather-bound notebook.

As far as the future looking bleak because of having only memories of Heather, that was becoming understandable, too. At the moment, he didn't have to settle for just memories. That was why they seemed totally inadequate.

But once he left Tucson and returned to his usual busy routine, the memories would take on greater significance.

"Double bingo," he said. "Damn, you're good, Marshall. You've got it all figured out."

After one last check of the room, Mack opened the door and left, enjoying his renewed sense of well-being.

That night, for the first time in his life, Mack dreamed about his father. In the dream, the man was so tall he towered over Mack, who seemed to be no more than inches high. His father's voice was like thunder, causing Mack to curl into a ball in an attempt to escape the threatening noise as his father loomed over him.

"You better listen to me, boy," his father bellowed. *"We're not like other people, and don't you forget it. We can't be tethered, not us Marshalls. We have to be free in order to live.*

"Don't fool yourself into thinking you can have

roots, a family, a woman to love until the day you die. That's not who we are.

"Are you listening to me, boy? If a woman tries to get her claws into you and keep you shackled, you hightail out of there. You're just like me. We have to be free and on the move. You'll live your life alone. Understand, boy? Alone...alone...alone—"

Mack sat bolt upright on the bed, immediately groaning from the pain that shot through his shoulder and down his arm from the sudden, rough movement.

He was drenched in sweat and his hands trembled as he dragged them down his face. He took a shuddering breath, then left the bed to get a pill for the hot pain that was beginning to consume his entire body.

When he returned to the bed, he willed himself to relax, to let the pill do its job so he could go back to sleep.

Alone...alone...alone, his mind echoed. Damn it, why had he had that dream? From the time he was in his early teens and could comprehend what his father continually harped about, he'd understood the message, accepted it, and had lived his life accordingly.

He had inherited a wanderlust gene from his father, and could not, would not, stay in one place for any length of time. He wasn't meant to have roots, a home, a wife and family, because he was his father's son.

He was alone, and he would always be alone.

The vivid image of a smiling Heather flitted across his mental vision, then settled in crystal clarity. She appeared so real, it was as though he could reach out and touch the soft skin of her cheek, slide his thumb over her lush lips.

But then the image began to fade, Heather's smile changed to a frown, then tears filled her eyes.

"No, Heather, wait," Mack said, lifting his right hand. "Please, don't go. Heather? Don't leave me alone and lonely and..." He dropped his arm heavily onto the bed and closed his eyes.

What was the matter with him? Mack thought, a chill sweeping through him. It was the pill. The drugs were really packing a punch this time.

He needed to just blank his mind and try to sleep, forget the dream, forget the tears that had shimmered in Heather's eyes, forget how empty and lonely he'd felt as she'd begun to disappear from his view.

Mack stared into the darkness and waited for sleep to take him into the oblivion he yearned for. But the first colorful streaks of dawn were lighting the sky before he finally slept.

During what Heather considered her lunch hour on Monday, she dashed to K mart and purchased a strapless bra and a pair of panty hose.

Her next stop was the used-clothing store where she always shopped, a smile of relief forming on her lips when she found a pair of evening sandals with tiny straps and a two-inch heel.

She then hurried through the grocery store, gathering what she needed to make Mack a home-cooked meal that night, having decided to not wait until after school and the added presence of the girls and their opinions about what should be served to Uncle Mack.

Her final errand was to tape a note on the front door of the house where the teenage girl, Becky, lived down the block, the message asking if she was free to baby-sit the twins on Friday night.

Back home Heather put away the groceries, made herself a peanut butter and jelly sandwich, poured a glass of milk, and settled in front of the computer, eating the simple lunch while she resumed working.

And through it all, she thought about Mack Marshall.

"Concentrate, Ms. Marshall," she said, frowning. "The IRS does not take kindly to errors, nor do your clients, so get it together."

She glanced quickly at the clock on the nightstand next to the bed.

She had so much work to do, she thought, and she wanted to wash her hair before Mack arrived for his home-cooked meal. She'd wear her hair falling free, not twist it into a braid, because Mack liked it that way, had said her hair was beautiful and—

"Aaak!" she yelled. "I'm over the edge. I'm losing my mind!"

She took a big bite of the gooey sandwich, narrowed her eyes and forced herself to study the numbers on the screen of the computer.

* * *

Just before five o'clock that evening Heather stood with a daughter on each side of her, the trio nodding in satisfaction as they scrutinized the kitchen table.

The girls had drawn pictures of bright flowers on construction paper to use as place mats and the crystal vase Mack had given Heather was in the center of the table, holding the few remaining flowers that hadn't wilted. Paper napkins had been folded into triangles, and plates, glasses and silverware were in place.

"I think the table looks lovely," Heather said. "Don't you?"

"It's very pretty," Emma said.

"Yep," Melissa said.

"If the place mats don't get soiled during dinner," Heather said, looking down at one daughter, then the other, "we can use them again for a farewell dinner when Uncle Mack leaves. Or you could make new ones for that event if you want to."

Melissa frowned. "Uncle Mack never *talks* about going away."

"Well," Heather said, "that's because we all know he's only here for a short while, so there's nothing more to say on the subject."

"Yes, there is," Emma said, folding her arms over her chest. "We can *say* we don't want Uncle Mack to leave, Mommy."

A knock at the front door saved Heather from having to respond to Emma's statement and Heather looked heavenward in gratitude. The twins ran to an-

PLAY THE
Lucky Key Game
and get

HOW TO PLAY:

1. With a coin, carefully scratch off gold area at the right. Then check the claim chart to see what we have for you — **2 FREE BOOKS** and a **FREE GIFT** — **ALL YOURS FREE!**

2. Send back the card and you'll receive two brand-new Silhouette Special Edition® novels. These books have a cover price of $4.50 each in the U.S. and $5.25 each in Canada, but they are yours to keep absolutely free.

3. There's no catch. You're under no obligation to buy anything. We charge nothing —ZERO — for your first shipment. And you don't have to make any minimum number of purchases — not even one!

4. The fact is, thousands of readers enjoy receiving books by mail from the Silhouette Reader Service™. They enjoy the convenience of home delivery...they like getting the best new novels at discount prices, BEFORE they're available in stores...and they love their *Heart to Heart* subscriber newsletter featuring author news, horoscopes, recipes, book reviews and much more!

5. We hope that after receiving your free books you'll want to remain a subscriber. But the choice is yours — to continue or cancel, any time at all! So why not take us up on our invitation, with no risk of any kind. You'll be glad you did!

YOURS FREE!
A SURPRISE MYSTERY GIFT

We can't tell you what it is...but we're sure you'll like it! A
FREE GIFT—
just for playing the LUCKY KEY game!

Visit us online at
www.eHarlequin.com

FREE GIFTS!

NO COST! NO OBLIGATION TO BUY!
NO PURCHASE NECESSARY!

PLAY THE
Lucky Key Game

Scratch gold area with a coin.
Then check below to see the gifts you get!

YES! I have scratched off the gold area. Please send me the 2 Free books and gift for which I qualify. I understand I am under no obligation to purchase any books, as explained on the back and on the opposite page.

| NAME | (PLEASE PRINT CLEARLY) |

| ADDRESS |

| APT.# | CITY |

| STATE/PROV. | ZIP/POSTAL CODE |

| 2 free books plus a mystery gift | 1 free book |
| 2 free books | Try Again! |

The Silhouette Reader Service™ — Here's how it works:

Accepting your 2 free books and gift places you under no obligation to buy anything. You may keep the books and gift and return the shipping statement marked "cancel." If you do not cancel, about a month later we'll send you 6 additional novels and bill you just $3.80 each in the U.S., or $4.21 each in Canada, plus 25¢ shipping & handling per book and applicable taxes if any.* That's the complete price and — compared to cover prices of $4.50 each in the U.S. and $5.25 each in Canada — it's quite a bargain! You may cancel at any time, but if you choose to continue, every month we'll send you 6 more books, which you may either purchase at the discount price or return to us and cancel your subscription.

*Terms and prices subject to change without notice. Sales tax applicable in N.Y. Canadian residents will be charged applicable provincial taxes and GST.

swer the door and Heather swept her gaze over the table one last time.

"That's as good as it gets," she said, shrugging. "It's the thought that counts."

And the endless thoughts of Mack that had consumed her mind the entire day, she mused as she walked slowly into the living room, what did *they* count for? What did they mean? Well, this certainly wasn't the time to attempt to figure it out.

"Hello, Mack." Heather smiled, then frowned in the next instant as she saw that the girls were each holding a brightly wrapped gift. "More presents?"

"For my hostesses," Mack said, extending a foil-covered box toward Heather. "Sweets for the sweet. How's that for corny?"

"Thank you," Heather said. "It was very thoughtful of you, but certainly not necessary. I wish you hadn't given the girls more—"

"Wow," Melissa said. "Look at this. A new baseball. A brand-new baseball. Thank you bunches, Uncle Mack. I can hardly wait to show Buzzy."

"Clothes for my Barbie doll?" Emma said, jumping up and down. "Oh...oh...oh, a wedding dress with a veil and a pair of shorts and a top and...oh, oh, thank you, thank you, Uncle Mack."

"You're most welcome," Mack said, smiling. "I hope you like chocolates, Heather."

"Mommy loves chocolates," Emma said. "One time she was baking us chocolate-chip cookies while we were at school, and she ate all the chocolate chips

before she baked the cookies, and we had chocolate chip
cookies with no chocolate chips, which was pretty weird,
but they really didn't taste so bad, I guess.''

"Thank you for sharing my deep dark secret,
Emma,'' Heather said dryly.

Mack laughed. "Well, it sounds like I picked the
right hostess gift for you, Heather.'' He took a deep
breath. "Ah, something smells delicious.''

"Chicken,'' Melissa said. "It's chicken that we
covered in corn flakes. I got to whop the corn flakes
in a bag until they were all crumbs and dusty stuff.''

"I'm sure you're a terrific corn flake whopper, Melissa,'' Mack said. "Top of the line.''

"There wasn't a line,'' Melissa said, cocking her
head to one side. "There was just me. The corn flakes
were my job and Emma gave the potatoes a bath.''

Heather laughed. "The descriptions of the prepa-
ration of this meal are lacking something. I suggest we
eat dinner before it loses its appeal. Off we go to the
kitchen, troops.''

The girls placed their gifts on the sofa, then ran
toward the kitchen. Heather set the box of candy on
the coffee table, then straightened and looked at Mack.

"Mack,'' she said quietly, "please stop bringing the
twins presents every time you come.''

"Why?'' he said, frowning. "It's a classic win-win
situation. I get a great deal of pleasure out of it and
so do they.''

"I realize that,'' Heather said, "but think about this.
Do you want them to be glad to see you, their Uncle

Mack, because they like to be with you, enjoy your company? Or do you want them to anticipate your arrival because it means they'll receive a materialistic reward? I, personally, prefer to be liked for me, the person, not for what I might have bought for someone.''

"Emma and Melissa aren't that shallow," Mack said, his voice rising slightly.

"Emma and Melissa are normal little six-year-old girls," Heather said. "If you keep this up, you're going to hear 'What did you bring me?' instead of 'I'm so glad to see you.' I don't want that to happen."

Mack nodded slowly.

"When you leave Tucson," Heather went on, "I want them to remember you as their special Uncle Mack, not as that neat guy who gave them tons of goodies. Do you understand what I'm saying?"

"Yes, I do. I'd like to compromise on this if we could. I'll ask you ahead of time before I buy them anything else. Does that sound feasible?"

"Yes, and thank you," Heather said, smiling. "Now then, are you ready for chicken covered in dusty corn flakes and baked potatoes that had a bath?"

"Sure." Mack paused. "Heather?"

"Yes?"

"How will *you* remember me when I leave Tucson?" Mack said, looking directly into her eyes.

As the man who made her feel incredibly feminine and alive, Heather thought, aware that her heart had increased its tempo. As the man who made her feel beautiful and special, cherished. As the man who caused desire like nothing she had ever known to sing throughout her body when he held and kissed her and—

"Mommy!" Melissa yelled from the kitchen.

Heather blinked, bringing her back from the hazy, sensuous place to which she had floated.

"I'll remember you as the man," she said, hearing the breathy quality of her voice, "who ate burned chicken at our table if we don't get into the kitchen."

Heather spun around and hurried across the room.

"We'll continue this discussion at a more appropriate time," Mack said, following her.

"No, we won't," Heather said, then shivered slightly as her response was answered with a very male, very rumbly chuckle.

The meal was placed on the table, grace was said, then lively chatter accompanied the consuming of the hot, delicious food. The menu was baked chicken coated in corn flake dust, potatoes baked after their bath and now slathered with butter and sour cream, corn, a tossed salad and chocolate brownies for dessert. Halfway through dinner a knock sounded at the front door.

"I'll get it," Heather said.

She hurried to the door and opened it to find Becky, who was holding the note Heather had taped to the front door of the teenager's house.

"Hi, Mrs. Marshall," Becky said. "I got your note about sitting for the twins on Friday night? But I have to, like, take care of my baby brother because my parents are going out, which is really a bummer because my folks don't even pay me? You know?

"So, I talked to my mom and, like, said it wasn't fair and all? And she said why didn't Emma and Melissa sleep over at our house on Friday? I could make puffy beds on the floor with blankets and stuff? Then I could get paid for taking care of the twins because I'm really broke?"

"Cool!" Melissa hollered from the kitchen. "Can we, Mom? That would be fun, Becky. You make awesome popcorn with lots of butter."

"Well..." Heather said.

"Please, Mom?" Emma yelled. "Then you could go out to dinner with Uncle Mack and wear your princess dress. But I like the popcorn you make with the cheese on it the best, Becky."

"The vote is in, Mom," Mack called. "Say yes."

Heather laughed. "Okay, okay, I give up."

"Majorly super," Becky said. "What time should I come collect the twins?"

"Seven o'clock," Mack yelled.

"Got it," Becky said. "Just, like, thanks a million. 'Bye."

"Goodbye, Becky." Heather closed the door, returned to the table and laughed as she sat down and spread her napkin on her lap. "Did you ever notice how a lot of teenagers end statements as though they were questions, Mack? You have to pay very careful attention to what they are saying so you know which ones you're really supposed to answer."

Mack stared into space. "I don't believe I've ever had a conversation with a teenager. Not that I recall, anyway." He looked at Heather. "But I did notice what you're talking about as I listened to Becky. Fascinating. I wonder why they do that?"

"I don't have a clue." Heather smiled. "My, my, aren't we subjecting you to all kinds of new experiences while you're visiting us?"

"Oh, yes, ma'am," Mack said, gazing at her intently. "You certainly are doing exactly that, Ms. Marshall, and some of those new experiences are etched indelibly in my mind."

A sliver of heat traveled down Heather's back, then swirled around to settle low in her body as she met Mack's mesmerizing gaze. She forced herself to shift her attention to the girls and told Melissa to drink her milk.

"I already finished my milk," Melissa said, obviously confused by her mother's directive.

"Oh, so you did," Heather said, then cleared her throat. "Silly me. Emma, drink your milk."

"Are you all right, Heather?" Mack said, an expression of pure innocence on his face. "You seem a bit...I don't know...flustered."

Heather glared at Mack. "You're not cute, Mr. Marshall. Not even close. Your clever little double-meaning statements are...are not cute."

"Buzzy's mom thinks Uncle Mack is cute," Melissa said. "She told me that. She said Uncle Mack is cute and a hunk of stuff, whatever that means. She saw his picture at the library, and then she looked out her window one time when Uncle Mack came to our house so she could see him really good, and she said she got the vipers.'' She shrugged. ''Or something like that.''

Mack hooted with laughter.

''The vapors,'' Heather said, smiling. ''Never mind, Melissa. Susie was just being funny.''

''No, she wasn't,'' Melissa said, '''cause she wasn't smiling one bit when she told me all that. Buzzy said he wished Uncle Mack was his daddy 'cause we get presents all the time from him and Buzzy's daddy doesn't even come to see him anymore since he went to live with that new mother he picked.''

''I see,'' Heather said, looking at Mack as she spoke. ''Do you girls think the gifts you've received are the best part of Uncle Mack visiting us?''

The twins looked at each other for a long moment, then directed their attention to their mother again.

''It's nice to get presents when it's not even your birthday,'' Emma said, ''but...'' She glanced at Melissa, who nodded. ''But it would be okay if Uncle Mack didn't bring us any more surprises, because me and Melissa talked about it together and we decided that the bestest thing would be if Uncle Mack was *our* daddy and could stay with us forever and ever.''

Chapter Eight

Heather and Mack stared at the twins with stunned expressions on their faces. In perfect unison they opened their mouths to reply, then snapped them closed again as neither could think of a response to Emma's statement, which seemed to hover heavily in the air.

Mack sank back in his chair and cleared his throat.

"Well, um, well, I..." he said, "I'm very...yes, *extremely* flattered that you girls would like me to be your father. That's a very nice compliment and I sincerely thank both of you."

"Will you do it, Uncle Mack?" Melissa said, leaning forward. "Be our daddy and stay with us forever and ever? You could live here with us until we get enough money in our dream piggy to buy our own house. You could sleep in Mommy's bed with her, because it's big enough for two people and she's only one mommy. See? Me and Emma figured everything out just fine.''

Heather plunked one elbow on the table and dropped her forehead into her palm. ''Oh, dear heaven,'' she said, ''I don't believe this.'' She raised her head again and looked at the twins. ''Emma, Melissa, I realize that you've given this a great deal of thought and have, in your minds, covered all the details but...please, you must listen to me. Uncle Mack is *not* going to be your daddy. He's your uncle and that's the only title he's going to have in regard to you two. Do you understand, girls? You've got to forget this idea of yours because it isn't going to happen, and you're just going to end up unhappy and disappointed if you continue to think it might come to be.''

''You're not being fair,'' Melissa yelled. ''You and Uncle Mack didn't even talk it over. It's not very nice that you don't want to share your bed with Uncle Mack when you know you have room to sleep with another person. How come you won't even think about it, Mommy? How come you won't talk to Uncle Mack about it before just saying no real fast?''

''Melissa, calm down and lower your voice,'' Heather said sternly. ''We don't holler in anger at each other in this house, young lady.''

''Sorry,'' Melissa mumbled, then folded her arms over her chest and glowered at her plate.

"But Melissa is right, Mom," Emma said. "You didn't even talk it over with Uncle Mack."

"Okay," Heather said, raising both hands in a gesture of peace. "I'll do that right now." She looked at Mack and lifted her chin. "Mack, as you are now aware, the twins have decided that you'd make a dandy daddy. However, as you have explained to us already, you are not the type of man who chooses to have roots, to settle in somewhere forever and ever. So, it is perfectly clear that you can't be the daddy around here because you won't even be in Tucson that much longer. Right?" Heather paused. "Mack? Hello? You and I are discussing this issue, remember? Would you please say something so we can get closure to this nonsense?"

"It's not nonsense," Melissa said, yelling again. "Sorry I screamed, but it's not dumb."

"Mack," Heather said, looking at him pointedly. "Speak, for Pete's sake."

He couldn't think clearly, Mack thought frantically, let alone say something intelligent. Images were slamming against his mind in a jumbled maze.

He saw himself in an enormous bed with Heather nestled close to his body, their heads resting on the same pillow.

He saw two sleep-tousled, smiling little girls appearing by the edge of the bed, then diving on top of it for morning hugs and tickles.

He saw them consuming breakfast, lunch, then dinner, as the four of them sat around this shabby table, love and laughter filling the small house to overflowing.

He saw a family. And he was an important part of it. The father. The husband. Forever and ever.

You'd better listen to me, boy. Don't fool yourself into thinking you can have roots, a family, a woman to love until the day you die. That's not who we are. You're just like me. We have to be free and on the move. You'll live your life alone. Understand, boy? Alone…alone…alone…

Mack squeezed his temples with his thumb and forefinger as his father's haunting words hammered at him, causing a sharp pain to throb in his head. He sucked in a shuddering breath, let it out slowly, then flattened his hand on the table top. Heather, Melissa and Emma were all staring at him intently.

"Your mother is right," he said, his voice slightly raspy. "I just…can't stay in one place for any length of time. I told you that, remember, girls? I wouldn't make a good father. I'm just not the man for the job.

"I think maybe I'm becoming a pretty decent uncle, but…" He shrugged. "But that's it, that's…that's all I'll ever be. Just…just your uncle Mack." Just Mack Marshall alone…alone…alone… "There. We've discussed it. Okay?"

What was wrong with Mack? Heather thought, still staring at him intently. He was obviously shaken, scrambling for the words that should have come so easily. The color had drained from his face and his voice sounded strange and—

Melissa sniffled. "'Kay. I guess."

"You could make being our daddy your dream, Uncle Mack," Emma said, her voice trembling. "You know you don't got a dream yet and…"

"Emma, honey, don't," Heather said gently. "You've got to accept the truth as it is, and just enjoy Uncle Mack's company while he's still here with us. Don't do this to yourself, sweetheart. There are some things in life that you just can't change. You and Melissa know that."

Emma sighed. "Yes, I know, but…"

"No," Heather said. "No more. We've discussed it and there's no more to say on the subject. Let's finish our dinners, then have those yummy chocolate brownies that are waiting for us."

"I'm not hungry anymore," Emma said.

"Me neither," Melissa said, "and I don't want any stupid brownies."

"Melissa, you're being rude," Heather said. "We invited Uncle Mack to share a home-cooked meal. Let's not spoil the occasion by being grumpy. We want Uncle Mack to remember this dinner with pleasant thoughts, don't we?"

"Yeah, I suppose," Melissa said, then picked up her fork. "And chocolate brownies aren't really stupid."

"That's better," Heather said, smiling. "Emma? Your fork, please?"

Emma did as instructed with a loud, dramatic sigh

and the consuming of the meal resumed. Quietly. Very, very quietly.

Heather concentrated on choking down the remainder of her dinner, keeping her eyes averted from Mack's.

You could make being our daddy your dream, Uncle Mack.

Emma's heartfelt words echoed in Heather's mind and she willed them to disappear, to leave her in peace. If Mack was the twins' daddy, that would mean he would be *her* husband...forever and ever. Oh, such a foolish notion. She had to listen to her own instructions to the girls and accept what could not be changed. *She knew that.*

Time after time in her life, to love, to believe in forever, had brought her heartache and tears. The pattern had been set in motion when she was still an infant, when her mother had abandoned her. Then her beloved grandmother had died, resulting in an endless series of goodbyes as she was shuffled from one foster home to the next.

She'd lowered her emotional guard when she'd met Frank Marshall, and where had that gotten her? Sobbing in the long, dark nights again, struggling to gather the pieces of her shattered heart.

Heather sighed inwardly and gave up the attempt to finish her dinner.

The bleak pattern of her existence had been broken once, just once, with the birth of her beautiful daughters. The love they all shared *was* forever and ever, and for that she was grateful beyond measure.

But she firmly believed that the blessing of the twins was all she was meant to have. It consumed the maternal section of her heart.

But the part of her that was just a woman? There was no forever-and-ever love for the woman within her. To love was to lose, to be abandoned, to cry in the night and to try desperately to hold together her heart that had once again been smashed to smithereens. That was just how it was, and the truth was etched in stone for all time. Yes, just like Melissa and Emma, she had to accept what could not be changed.

And she had.

And would continue to do so.

So, no, she thought, sliding a quick glance at Mack, even if whatever was steadily growing between her and Mack Marshall grew even more, then blossomed into love, she wouldn't embrace that emotion. No. She would ignore it, allow it to dim, then die from lack of nurturing, because never again—*never*—was she going to cry in the dark, lonely night, then search for the scattered fragments of her broken heart.

"Well," Heather said, forcing a lightness to her voice that she definitely didn't feel, "I think everyone's tummy is full. Shall we have the brownies later? Yes, that's a good idea. Would you girls like to go out front and play while I clean up the kitchen?"

"'Kay," Melissa said, sliding off of her chair.

"Can I go to Buzzy's and show him my new base-ball?"

"Yes, you may," Heather said. "Invite Buzzy to play catch in our yard. Emma, you can sit on the carpet square under the tree and try the new clothes on your Barbie doll. It's a lovely evening. Uncle Mack and I will get the lawn chairs and join you out front. In fact, you could do that now, Mack."

"No, I'll help you put away the food," he said.

"That's not necessary," Heather said, still not looking at him. "You're our guest tonight."

Emma got to her feet. "Do you want to come outside now, Uncle Mack?"

"No, I'll wait for your mother," he said.

"'Kay," Emma said. "Come on, Melissa."

The girls hurried out of the kitchen and Heather got to her feet quickly, picking up plates as she moved.

"You just sit right there where you are, Mack," she said. "This chore will be completed faster if I do it alone, because I have a set routine, know where everything goes. I'm...I'm accustomed to being alone and...and that's fine, just fine. Yes, alone is good because..."

Mack pushed back his chair, got to his feet, and took the plates from Heather's hands. She slowly, very slowly, met his gaze.

"Heather," Mack said quietly, "I'm sorry, so damn sorry. You must be furious with me, even wishing that I'd never searched for you, found you, because I've upset your daughters, brought them close to tears.

"I feel like a villain because my presence here gave the twins a false hope that...just being their Uncle Mack isn't enough and that's very humbling, believe me. I sincerely apologize for disrupting the peaceful existence you had with your girls. If you want me to leave Tucson tonight, I will. It's up to you and I'll do whatever you decide is best."

No! Heather thought, icy panic rushing through her. She didn't want Mack to leave. Not yet. She wasn't prepared to say goodbye to him. Not yet. Oh, no, Mack, please, not yet.

Heather took the plates back from Mack, carried them to the counter, then plunked them down. She turned to meet his troubled gaze.

"If parents...that is, if *people* headed for the hills," she said, "every time children cornered them with something that was difficult or uncomfortable to deal with, those adults wouldn't be home very much."

"But..."

"No, please, hear me out," Heather said, raising one hand. "The girls presented their plan. We, you and I, discussed it, then gave them an answer. They didn't like what they heard, but they *will* accept it, just as they have other challenges they've presented to me in the past.

"You certainly don't have to leave Tucson earlier than you planned because the twins are momentarily upset, Mack. As the old cliché goes, 'This, too, shall pass.' End of story."

"Are you sure?" Mack said, frowning.

"Trust me," Heather said. "Now then, if you'll sit down out of my way, I'll have this kitchen cleaned in a jiffy and we can go outside and enjoy a lovely spring evening."

Mack nodded, then sank onto one of the chairs at the table, absently rubbing his left shoulder as he stared into space. Several minutes went by in total silence as Heather cleared the table and loaded the dishwasher.

"Of course, there's another side to this coin, Mack," Heather said finally as she began to place left-overs in plastic containers. "Maybe you'd *prefer* to leave Tucson now. You're under no obligation to weather this temporary emotional storm the girls have stirred up."

Mack snapped his head around to look at Heather. "No," he said much too loudly. "Sorry. I didn't mean to bark at you, but leaving earlier than I planned isn't even close to what I want to do."

"Well, then," Heather said, shrugging. "That settles it, doesn't it?" She paused. "Just how long do you see yourself staying? You've been rather vague about it."

Mack glanced at the calendar on his watchband. "I'm supposed to see the doctor in New York about my shoulder two weeks from tomorrow. He's not too thrilled with me that I left the city in the first place, so…well, I guess I'd fly out two weeks from today so I'd be there on time for the appointment."

"I see," Heather said quietly. "Is your shoulder healing properly?"

"I don't have a clue," he said, leaning back in the chair. "I've never been shot before, which is a miracle when I really stop and think about it. I'm fortunate to be alive when I look back at some of the ridiculous risks I took to take a photograph I was so damn determined to have." He shook his head. "It always seemed like a good idea at the time."

Heather stacked the paper place mats on the end of the counter, then began to wipe off the table.

"You sound as though you're a bit angry at yourself for how you've operated in the past," she said. "Those risks earned you many awards and worldwide recognition. That's got to be worth a great deal to you."

"Oh, I don't know, Heather." Mack sighed. "This isn't the proper time for me to be examining my life, I suppose. I'm not up to par physically and I'm so tired of the pain this wound is causing. I'm just worn out. Let's change the subject. I must be coming across as a whiny kid."

Her chores completed, Heather sat at the table, opposite Mack.

"No, you aren't," she said, meeting Mack's gaze directly. "Not that you asked, but I personally think this *is* a good time to take a hard look at your existence, to decide if you want to continue to lay your life on the line. Once your wound is healed, you might just go on as before, sort of set on automatic." She smiled. "How's that for not minding my own business?"

"I value your opinion," Mack said, "and I'll definitely think about what you just said. Hey, you've got one coming as far as minding my business. I'm the guy who told you to wear your hair falling free like it is now, instead of in a braid. Now *that's* pushy." He reached over and sifted some of Heather's hair through his fingers. "But it really is beautiful. A silky, ebony waterfall."

"Thank you," Heather said, hardly above a whisper.

Mack slowly, very slowly, withdrew his hand from her hair and flattened his palm on the table.

"Why have you worn your hair loose since I asked you to?" he said.

"Oh, well, I..." Heather started, then frowned and stopped speaking. "No, let's be honest here. I'm a woman, not just a mother. I like feeling beautiful and feminine, even though it's for a short time. And when I wear my princess dress on Friday night, I'm going to be..." She laughed. "...so gorgeous just like Cinderella was after being visited by the fairy godmother."

"There you go," Mack said, matching her smile. "Whew. Talk about pressure. I've got to measure up to being a Prince Charming on Friday night."

"No-o-o-o problem," Heather said. "After all, we already know that you're cute *and* a hunk of stuff because Susie said so. I think that puts you in the princely department.''

Mack chuckled, then became serious in the next moment. He reached across the table and covered Heather's left hand with his right.

''You're an incredible woman, Heather Marshall,'' he said, his voice low and rumbly. ''You're so honest and real and...you have tremendous fortitude, inner strength, yet you're gentle and...I like you very, very much, and care about you, what happens to you. I want you to be happy, to have your dream of owning a home come true, because you deserve that and much more. I'm very grateful that I found you, Heather.''

Oh, gracious, Heather thought frantically, she was about to cry. Mack sincerely meant every word he was saying. She knew he did because of the expression on his face and the emotions shining in the depths of his dark, compelling eyes.

He had just praised her as a person, a woman, and she was going to wrap it all around her like a warm, comforting blanket that she could reach for when he was gone, when her day-to-day responsibilities became cold and heavy.

''I...I like you, too, Mack Marshall,'' she said, hoping her voice was steady. ''And I care about what happens to you in the future.'' She managed to produce a small smile. ''I'd really appreciate it if you didn't get shot again because I don't have time in my busy schedule to have a nervous breakdown worrying about you.''

"Oh, okay," he said, releasing her hand and folding his arms over his chest. "I'll cross getting shot off my agenda." He shook his head. "Believe me, it's not something I'd ever want to repeat. That thing about your life passing before your eyes is true when you think you're about to die. Well, it was for me, at least.

"Oh, sweet Heather, you continually give me the gift of your honesty when we talk. I'm going to tell you something that is straight from my heart, completely honest, something I didn't think I'd ever tell another living soul because it...it's wimpy, about as far from machismo as a guy can get."

Heather nodded. "I'm listening."

"When I was shot," he said, his voice gritty, "I knew that I sure as hell didn't want to die there in the dirt in that godforsaken place. What was really ripping me up, causing the darkest depression I've ever experienced, was the fact that if I *did* die..." He stopped to take a shuddering breath.

"If you did die...what?" Heather said gently, her heart aching as she saw the flicker of raw pain cross Mack's features then settle into his eyes.

"If I died," he said, "no one...no one...would...no one would cry."

"Oh, Mack," Heather said, unable to keep tears from filling her eyes.

"That's why I had to find you, don't you see?" he said. "Find you, the girls, my family. I had to know that there was at least a chance... God, this is weird...but I had to know that someone would cry if I died.''

He stared up at the ceiling for a long moment to regain control of his raging emotions, then looked at Heather again. ''I can't believe I just told you that, but...but I'm glad I did because...hell, I don't know why I'm glad I shared that with you. Ho-boy, I think I'm actually slipping over the edge of my sanity here.''

''I'm very honored that you told me,'' Heather said softly. ''And I understand, I truly do, what you were saying, how you felt at that moment when you believed you were going to die. I've been completely alone in this world in the past and it's so empty, chilling, so very stark.

''At different points in my life if I had disappeared off the face of the earth, if I had died, there would have been no one...no one to cry. That is loneliness with a depth so deep it's hard to describe.

''Now? I have my daughters and we'll love one another forever and ever, unconditionally. God forbid that something should happen to me, but if it did, Melissa and Emma would miss me, they would cry.''

Mack nodded.

''You're not alone anymore, Mack,'' Heather went on. ''You have a family now. If you...died, the girls would be devastated, would most definitely cry about the loss of their wonderful Uncle Mack. I hope that knowing that brings you some comfort.''

''It does, believe me,'' he said. ''And you, Heather? Would you cry if I died?''

A sudden image of a shadowy cemetery flashed in Heather's mental vision and she saw herself staring at a headstone with tears streaming down her face.

''Yes,'' she whispered. ''I would cry.''

Heather and Mack looked at each other. What should have been a gloomy moment, the talk of death, of mourning, was instead a sharing, growing moment of greater understanding, of baring souls and telling secrets they knew would be safely kept. It was a moment that caused a gentle warmth to consume them. It was a moment that would never be forgotten.

But then the warmth shifted, changed, became the now-familiar heat of desire, churning within them, building, causing hearts to race and breaths to quicken.

''Ah, Heather,'' Mack said, breaking the crackling silence, ''I want you so damn much. Maybe you don't wish to hear that, but sitting here we've been so honest with each other that I have to tell you how very, very much I desire you, and want to make love with you.''

''I...''

''No, you don't have to say anything,'' he said, shaking his head. ''I'm not pushing you about it. I...''

''Mom!'' Melissa yelled in the distance.

Heather jerked in her chair at the sudden loud noise, then shifted to turn toward the living room.

''Yes, Melissa?'' she called. ''What is it?''

''Are you and Uncle Mack coming outside soon? Buzzy and his mom are here, and Grandma Hill, and

Mr. and Mrs. Garcia, and…and just everybody from the block came over to meet our Uncle Mack and…guess what?…they want his autograph! Isn't that really cool?''

Mack groaned and rolled his eyes heavenward.

"We'll be right there, Melissa," Heather said.

"'Kay," Melissa hollered. "I'll tell 'em."

Heather laughed as she got to her feet. "Your public awaits, sir. You mustn't disappoint your fans. You're probably very accustomed to it, but isn't it at least a little bit exciting that people want your autograph?"

"Not really," Mack said, rising. "It's *never* made any sense to me why someone would want a person's name scrawled on a piece of paper. It's a very strange custom."

"But it's part of the world you exist in," Heather said as they started toward the front door.

"I suppose," Mack said.

A world, Heather thought, as a dark cloud seemed to settle above her, that was far, far away from this shabby little street in Tucson, Arizona.

Chapter Nine

Early Friday evening Mack stood in front of the mirror in the bathroom in his hotel room and shaved for a second time that day.

A princess, he decided, should not go to a fancy restaurant escorted by a would-be prince with a five-o'clock shadow.

He began to hum off-key as he pulled the razor through the foam on his cheeks.

It had been a great week, he thought, and he really liked the people who lived on Heather's street and made up the pseudo family she adored.

Mack replayed the previous days in his mind as he continued to shave.

Monday night's impromptu block party set a delightful pattern for the week.

On Tuesday, Mack took Heather, the twins and Buzzy to a fast-food restaurant for hamburgers, then they returned to the house where Mack and Heather sat in lawn chairs while the children played in the yard. The neighbors wandered down the street to join them, chairs in tow, and lively conversation took place until it was bath and bedtime for the kids.

Wednesday night found the Marshalls eating dinner at Grandma Hill's, with the neighborhood gathering taking place later in the older woman's front yard.

Susie hosted a potluck dinner on Thursday evening. She made a huge pot of spaghetti, while contributions of tossed salad, crusty loaves of bread, iced tea, ice cream and cookies resulted in a delicious meal that everyone thoroughly enjoyed.

Through the entire week, Mack mused on, he'd taken endless pictures, the neighbors soon becoming accustomed to the whirring sound of his camera. He had everyone sign releases in case he decided to use any of the photographs professionally in the future, a request that resulted in Melissa and Buzzy wearing sunglasses just like, they stated, movie stars.

Yep, Heather's neighbors were good people. They were hardworking, honest and real, and all of them, he'd soon discovered, had a dream. They yearned for a better life beyond the shabby area where they now lived, wanted more for their children than they presently had, saw the future as filled with hope, not as an endless stretch of bleak, hand-to-mouth days.

After Monday evening's autograph session, his celebrity status was pushed aside as unimportant, and he was accepted for who he was as a man. No one resented his wealth and success, he had realized from conversations that took place. They simply viewed him as someone who had worked hard, sacrificed whatever had been necessary, and achieved his goals in his chosen profession.

It was a totally new experience to be with people who wanted nothing from him but his company for a few hours, Mack thought as he began to dress.

He had been more relaxed and at ease with Heather's friends than he ever was at the high-society functions he'd attended around the world. At those affairs he'd always stayed on guard, waiting for the reason someone had sought him out, listening carefully for the bottom line that would tell him what the person hoped to gain by being seen, or photographed, with the famous Mack Marshall.

Mack went back to the mirror in the bathroom and knotted his tie.

Heather, his mind hummed. She was an intricate part of the *family* on her block, and was sincerely loved by all. His respect for her had grown even greater during the past week, if that was possible, and so had his depth of caring. Heather was rare and wonderful, and so beautiful that it sometimes took his breath away as he drank in the sight of her laughing and talking with her neighbors, or kissing the twins good night after listening to their prayers.

Mack glanced at his watch, then wandered into the large living room of the suite.

He was ready far too early, he knew, as he sat on the sofa, but he'd been counting down the hours to this special Cinderella night with Heather when she would wear her princess dress.

As much as he'd enjoyed the entire week, there had been no real opportunity to be alone with Heather, other than to kiss her goodbye in her living room at the end of each evening.

Kisses that had caused heated desire to rocket throughout his body the instant his lips met the lush sweetness of hers.

Kisses that had resulted in him tossing and turning through the long hours of the night until the light of dawn announced the beginning of a new day.

But tonight? Tonight was theirs, his and Heather's.

Mack got to his feet and began to pace restlessly around the room.

This was ridiculous, he fumed. He was actually nervous about the evening ahead, was tensing up, causing his shoulder to ache.

He, Jet Set Marshall, who had been shown in photographs on the society pages of newspapers around the globe with an endless stream of gorgeous women on his arm, was jangled, coming unglued, about taking Heather Marshall to a fancy restaurant.

But, damn, he wanted this evening to be perfect down to the most minute detail for Heather, to really be a Cinderella night for her. She deserved to feel special and beautiful because...well, because she was.

Mack halted his trek and looked at his watch again, his gaze falling on the calendar on the band.

He only had a little more than a week left to stay in Tucson, he thought, frowning. Time was passing too quickly, too damn fast.

He'd like to forget about that doctor's appointment he had in New York, but that would be foolish. The physician was a specialist, who was determined that the nerves and muscles in Mack's shoulder would be as good as new once the wound completely healed.

Coming to Tucson against the man's orders had already pushed the limits of sensibility. To ignore the scheduled checkup would be putting too much at risk as far as regaining full, pain-free mobility of his arm.

But, damn it, he thought, hooking one hand over the back of his neck, he didn't want to leave Heather. He didn't want to get on a plane with nothing more than memories of Heather, Melissa and Emma.

Cripe, listen to him. He was pitching a fit about the way things were, needed to be lectured by Heather as the twins had been about accepting things that could not be changed.

He was who he was...his father's son, a man with a wanderlust spirit and the need to be on the move. He just wasn't capable of settling down and settling in. Even if he fell in love with Heather, which he had no intention of doing, he would have to ignore that powerful emotion because he couldn't be for her what she deserved to have.

Melissa and Emma, he knew, were convinced that their uncle Mack could learn to be a tree with roots, could be taught the rules of how to be part of a family, could be their daddy and stay with them and their mom forever and ever.

But that wasn't going to happen. He would get on that plane with his memories tucked safely in his heart and wing his way back to New York with a sketchy plan to visit Heather and the girls again in the future. He'd leave knowing he had a family in Tucson who cared about him, people who would cry if he died.

So be it. That had been the goal of this journey...to find and connect with Heather Marshall and her daughters. He'd accomplished his objective and that was that. In a handful of days he'd be gone.

It was all just as it should be, Mack thought, but, damn it, why did the image of leaving cause a cold fist to tighten in his gut and the days and nights ahead loom dark and lonely in his mind?

Ah, hell, enough of this. He was mentally rambling, killing time until he could pick up Heather, and he was depressing himself for some unknown reason. So right now he was shifting into his Prince Charming mode so that Cinderella would have a fantastic evening, the stuff of which special and cherished memories were made.

Memories. In a little more than a week, that was all he and Heather would have...memories.

"Marshall," he said, grabbing his jacket off the back of a chair, "give it a rest. There's a beautiful lady wearing a princess dress waiting for you to create a magical night for her, bud. Don't blow it."

Heather moved in front of the full-length mirror in her bedroom and closed her eyes for a moment before looking at her reflection. She opened her eyes again slowly, and they widened at what she saw.

"Oh, my," she whispered.

The dress was exquisite, she thought, swaying and watching the lush material float around her like a peach-colored cloud. The lace camisole was, well, quite sexy, with thin lace straps and an enticing glimpse of her breasts that pushed above the strapless bra beneath the soft material.

She looked like a princess, she really did, with her shiny, fresh-washed hair tumbling down her back, a light touch of makeup, and a sparkle of excitement and anticipation about the evening ahead that even she could see in her dark eyes.

"I'm Cinderella," she said merrily, "and my prince is on his way to whisk me off for a fairy-tale night."

Her prince? she thought, in the next instant. Well, yes, he was...for now, for the time remaining until Mack left Tucson, the week and two days until he boarded that plane and flew away, perhaps never to return.

Don't go there, Heather told herself firmly. Not

now, not tonight. She wasn't going to have one gloomy thought on this glorious Cinderella night.

"Mom!" Melissa yelled from the living room. "Becky is here to get us."

"I'm coming," Heather answered, then picked up a small purse and left the bedroom.

When she entered the living room, Melissa, Emma and Becky stopped talking to one another and stared at Heather with wide eyes.

"Wow," Becky said. "You look awesome, Mrs. Marshall. Like, you know, I've never seen you in a dress before? And...wow."

Emma clasped her hands beneath her chin and sighed. "Oh, you really are a princess, Mommy. A beautiful princess."

"Don't those shoes hurt your toes?" Melissa said, frowning. "The dress is pretty good, but those shoes are kinda weird."

"These are princess shoes, Melissa," Heather said, smiling. "They're not allowed to pinch my toes. It's against the rules of being shoes for a princess."

"Oh-h-h," Melissa said, nodding. "'Kay. That's cool. But I'm sure glad kids don't have to wear shoes like those. Nope. Not me."

"Come on, you guys," Becky said. "My folks want to get going to dinner and a movie and I have to give my baby brother a bath, you know?"

"Are we still having popcorn?" Melissa said.

"Yep," Becky said. "Two kinds? Butter and cheese? Say goodbye to your mom, the princess."

Hugs and kisses were exchanged, then the trio left the house, the twins carrying their sleep-over supplies in grocery sacks. As they exited, Heather heard them greet Mack, and felt a bevy of butterflies flutter instantly through her stomach.

"Get it together, Cinderella," she told herself, but for the life of her she could not produce a smile as Mack entered the living room.

Heather stood statue-still, hardly breathing, drinking in the very sight of Mack, who stood just inside the closed door staring at her intently, no readable expression on his face.

Oh, look at her Prince Charming, Heather thought, rather giddily. In a tan suit with a chocolate-brown shirt and tan tie, he was magnificent. The suit was obviously custom-made, fitting him to perfection, making his shoulders appear wider, his legs more powerful, his tan deeper and his thick, black hair beckoning to have feminine fingers woven through it.

She was Cinderella, the princess, and Mack was the prince and this was their night, a page out of a fairy tale, a world away from reality.

"You are the most beautiful woman I have ever seen," Mack said quietly, bringing Heather from her whimsical thoughts. "You look sensational, Heather. You're truly a princess."

"For tonight," she said, her smile genuine. "You're a very handsome prince, too, Mack." She paused. "Thank you for making this evening possible. I've never felt so special and...I sincerely thank you."

"Believe me, Heather," he said, "the pleasure is mine." He extended his right hand toward her. "Shall we go, Princess?"

Heather took a steadying breath, then crossed the room to place her hand in Mack's. Their eyes met for a long, heart-stopping moment, then matching warm smiles formed on their lips as they left the house, each anticipating the hours ahead that were theirs alone to share.

Mack had spoken at length with the concierge at his hotel regarding the availability of four- and five-star restaurants in Tucson, and when he entered the selected establishment with Heather, he made a mental note to circle back later and give the concierge a sizable tip.

As they stood by the hostess's podium, waiting to be seated, Mack looked at Heather, who was sweeping her gaze over the large room. His heart seemed to swell in his chest as he saw the awe and wonder on her face, the sparkle of excitement in her big, dark eyes and the lovely flush on her cheeks.

"What do you think?" he said. "Is this place fit for a princess?"

"Oh, Mack," she said, looking up at him, "it's like something in a movie. I've never been anywhere so...so glamorous, so romantic and...I'm not sure I believe I'm really here."

"You *deserve* to be here," he said firmly. "This is your...yes, your castle, where you belong."

Heather laughed in delight. "How marvelous. I have crystal chandeliers in my castle and candles glowing on tables with pretty cloths, and fine china, and waiters in tuxedos. Can you believe that? The waiters are actually wearing tuxedos to serve the food."

The hostess approached them. "Your table is ready. If you'll follow me, please?"

Would everyone they passed notice, Heather thought, that the woman in the lovely peach dress wasn't walking next to the handsome man in the tan suit, but was floating on a mystical cloud?

They were seated at a small table and handed large, flocked menus. There were no prices listed on hers, Heather noted as Mack selected a wine. When it arrived, Mack performed the tasting ritual and declared it to be excellent. The wine steward filled their glasses, set the bottle on the table, then nodded and hurried away.

Mack lifted his glass and Heather did the same.

"May all your dreams come true," he said, touching his glass to Heather's.

"And may you find a dream for yourself and have it come true," she said.

They took a sip of the smooth wine, looking at each other over the top of the crystal glasses, then placed them on the linen cloth, their gazes still meeting.

The room around them faded into oblivion, along with the muted sounds of voices and dishes being stacked and removed somewhere in the distance.

They were alone in the glorious castle, Princess Cinderella and Prince Charming. Desire began to weave back and forth between them and they welcomed it, allowing it to consume them, to bring smoky hues to dark eyes and soft smiles to their lips.

It was their night. A magical night. A night of memories to keep for all time.

Everything was absolutely perfect, Heather decided. The food was hot and delicious, the service impeccable, the conversation flowed easily from one fascinating subject to the next. They lingered over after-dinner coffee and rich brandy in wafer-thin snifters.

"The twins are probably asleep by now," Mack said, "but I hope they enjoyed their evening with Becky and the butter and cheese popcorn."

"Shh," Heather said, placing a finger lightly against her lips for a moment. "You mustn't speak the names of the little princesses or you'll disturb the visions of sugar plums dancing in their slumbering heads."

"Ah, I see," Mack said, smiling. "In other words, you're not putting on your mommy hat tonight."

"No, I'm not," Heather said. "Is that terrible of me to not want to get into an in-depth discussion about Melissa and Emma?"

"Not at all. You have every right to take the night off from that role." Mack chuckled. "Hey, you don't see a camera hanging around my neck, do you? This evening I'm just Mack Marshall, not Mack Marshall the photojournalist. We all need to be ourselves for a while, with no titles tacked on the back of our name.''

''Thank you,'' Heather said, laughing. ''Now I don't have to feel guilty. I'm not Heather the mommy, nor the accountant, I'm just Heather the woman for these stolen hours, and shame on me, but it feels wonderful.''

''I'm glad you're enjoying yourself.''

''Oh, I am, Mack,'' she said, smiling at him warmly.

''So am I, believe me,'' he said.

The waiter came to the edge of the table. ''Will there be anything else this evening?''

''Heather?'' Mack said.

''No, thank you,'' she said.

''That's it for tonight,'' Mack said to the man.

''Very good, sir,'' the waiter said, then placed a leather folder on the table.

As Mack retrieved a credit card from his wallet and tended to the bill, Heather sighed inwardly. Well, Cinderella, she thought, the clock is about to strike midnight and end this glorious outing.

She glanced at her watch.

Well, she mused, she'd been allowed more time than the original Cinderella as it was already after midnight, but the hours with Mack had just flown by and the wondrous evening was ending too soon. *Too soon.*

''Ready to go?'' Mack said, pushing back his chair and getting to his feet.

No! Heather thought. It's too soon.

"Yes, fine," she said, rising as Mack assisted her with her chair.

Ten minutes later they were in Mack's vehicle and moments after that he was driving through the heavy, Friday night traffic. Heather looked out the passenger side window, silently willing Mack to drive slower, and mentally telling every green light to switch to red as they approached.

She turned her head to gaze at Mack as he concentrated on driving, and a soft smile formed on her lips as she drank in the sight of him in the changing colors of the signs they passed.

So magnificent, Heather mused. Mack's blatant masculinity was filling the vehicle to overflowing, his sensuality reaching out to stroke her, fanning the embers of desire that had been glowing within her all evening into hot, leaping flames that were consuming her.

Dear heaven, how she wanted this man.

What would it be like to be the recipient of all that power and strength that she knew, just somehow knew, would be tempered with infinite gentleness, was beyond the scope of even her wildest imagination.

"Your chariot has returned you safely to your home, Cinderella," Mack said, parking in front of Heather's house and turning off the ignition.

"That," Heather said, glancing at the little house, "is *not* a castle."

"Nope, but someday you'll have your dream, a home of your very own."

"Yes," Heather said. "That dream will come true no matter what sacrifices are needed to make it a reality. There are times when I'm so very tired that I cling to that thought like a lifeline."

"Don't ever give up on your dream, Heather. I envy you the fact that you have it."

Before Heather could reply, Mack got out of the vehicle and came around to assist her from the passenger side.

Heather had left one lamp lit in the living room and the soft glow greeted them when they entered the house. Heather walked to the middle of the room, then turned to see that Mack was still standing by the closed door.

"I had a wonderful time," she said. "Saying thank you for this evening isn't enough, but...please know that I won't ever forget feeling like a princess while with my Prince Charming."

"You're very welcome," Mack said. "I won't forget this night, either." He shook his head and pulled the knot of his tie down several inches. "Heather, I'm not going to kiss you good night because I'm hanging on by a thread here. I want you so damn much and I don't want to run the risk of losing control, frightening you in any way or... I've got to go. Right now."

"I thought you said that some risks in life are worth taking," Heather said.

"Yes, well..." Mack turned and placed one hand on the doorknob.

"Mack."

He looked over his shoulder at Heather questioningly.

"Yes?"

She took a steadying breath, then lifted her chin. "I'm not ready to give back my title of princess, not yet. It's too soon. This is a magical night, *our* night, created just for the two of us. I...I want you, Mack. I want to make love with you very, very much."

Chapter Ten

The echo in Mack's ears from his pounding heart was so loud that he shook his head slightly before attempting to speak.

"Are you certain about this, Heather?" he said finally, his voice gritty.

"Oh, yes," she said softly. "You've said all along that this is my choice to make, but now the decision rests in your hands. Do you want me, Mack? Do you want to end this magical night by making love with me?"

"You know I do, but..." Mack stopped speaking and frowned. "I just have to be sure that you won't have any regrets, that you won't be hurt or upset or...I couldn't handle it if I was the cause of your being unhappy, Heather. I really couldn't."

"I won't regret what we share on this night, Mack. I promise you that," Heather said. "I really don't expect you to understand, but for these hours I am a woman, just a woman, nothing more.

"That's a gift you've given to me, along with my princess dress. I'm going to wrap up these memories and tuck them carefully away so I can cherish them, because I may never again have stolen time when I'm just a woman."

Mack nodded and moved toward Heather slowly, his gaze meeting hers in the soft glow of the lamp. A shiver of anticipation swept through her as he came closer, closer, then stopped in front of her and cradled her face in his hands.

Mack held Heather's gaze for another long moment, then lowered his head and brushed his lips over hers, once, twice, then captured her mouth in a searing kiss.

Heather, his mind hummed as heated desire rocketed through him. On this night, this incredible night, he was going to make love with his rare, and beautiful, and wonderful Heather. It had to be perfect for her, worthy of being a cherished memory. *Ah, Heather.*

Mack broke the kiss and took a ragged breath.

"Mack, wait," Heather said, her voice trembling with desire. "Your shoulder. I was so centered on what *I* wanted that I didn't think about the fact that maybe you shouldn't—"

"Shh," he said. "Don't worry about my shoulder. It will be fine." He smiled. "I think we'd better go into your bedroom before we end up not making it that far.''

"You're right," Heather said, matching his smile. "After all, Melissa said I had plenty of room in my big bed and she couldn't understand why I wasn't willing to share it with you."

Mack chuckled. "I don't think we'll tell her that you came around to her way of thinking on the subject."

"No."

"I'd like to be very romantic here and carry you down the hall, but I do believe my shoulder would object to that one."

Heather stepped back and took Mack's left hand in her right.

"We'll walk side by side," she said. "Equal partners." She paused. "No, that's not quite true. I'm certainly not an *equal* partner as far as experience in…in this sort of thing. Frank is the only man I've ever been with, and so many years have passed, and…oh, dear."

Mack dropped a quick kiss on Heather's lips.

"Neither of us has a past as of this moment," he said. "This is a magical night, remember? It's ours."

"No past. No future. Just now," Heather said, nodding. "Yes, that's exactly how it is."

"Well, I…" Mack started, then hesitated, feeling strangely chilled by Heather's words. He mentally pushed away the disturbing feeling. "You're right. That's exactly how it is."

"Come with me, my Prince Charming," Heather said, tightening her hold on Mack's hand.

"I'm right here by your side, Cinderella."

Once they reached Heather's room, she snapped on the small lamp on the computer table, casting soft shadows over the expanse. Mack swept back the blankets on the bed, then turned to see Heather reach behind her to unzip the peach-colored dress. It fell to the floor, she stepped free of it, then began to remove the remainder of her clothes.

Mack removed his own clothes by rote and tossed them on the chair by the computer, his gaze riveted on Heather, blood pounding in his veins as he drank in the exquisite sight of her.

They stood in front of each other, naked, offering freely all that they were.

"Ah, Heather," Mack said, his voice gritty, "you are so...so lovely, so beautiful." He closed the distance between them and sifted his hands through her lush, dark hair, bringing it forward and watching it slide through his fingers to fall over her breasts. "Incredible."

Heather frowned as she looked at the angry red scar and puckered skin on Mack's shoulder. She leaned forward and kissed the wound lightly.

"I hate the idea that you were hurt so badly," she said. "I wish I could kiss it and make it better."

"You just did."

Heather smiled at him warmly, then moved onto the center of the bed. Mack stared at her, etching every inch of her indelibly in his mind as if she were a photograph he knew he would keep for all time, then he settled next to her and his mouth melted over hers.

The night was theirs.

And it was magic.

The awkwardness caused by Mack's attempt to keep too much weight off his left arm and Heather being certain she didn't grip his damaged shoulder did nothing to diminish the ecstasy of what they were sharing.

They kissed and caressed, discovered and marveled in the mysteries of each other, gave and received and gloried in it all.

Mack took the soft flesh of one of Heather's breasts deep into his mouth, laving the nipple with his tongue. She closed her eyes to fully savor each heated sensation that thrummed throughout her. He moved to the other breast to pay equal homage and she sank her fingers into his thick, black hair, urging him to take more, take her, all of her.

They were on fire, burning with need, hearts racing and the name of the other whispering from lips that were never still.

Mack left Heather only long enough to take steps to protect her, then returned to the welcoming warmth of her embrace, aching with the want of her, telling himself over and over that this must be perfect for her. Perfect for his Heather.

"Mack, please," Heather said, a sob of need catching in her throat. "I want you so much."

He moved over her, entering her slowly, watching her face for any sign that he was hurting her, acutely aware that it had been a very long time since she'd been with a man. But Heather raised her hips and a groan rumbled in Mack's chest.

"No, don't," he said. "I don't want to rush you, hurt you, or—"

"Shh," she said, pressing her hands on the small of his back. "Come to me, Mack. I'm waiting for you. All of you. Please."

And Mack was lost. He tipped over the edge of reason and reality and filled her with all that he was. He began to move, the tempo quickening instantly, then becoming a raging rhythm that Heather met beat for beat.

The night was theirs.

And it was magic.

Heather and Mack were one.

The sensual tension within them coiled tighter, hotter, as they neared the climax of their joining, their journey to a place they could go to only together. Tighter, hotter, higher, then flinging them over the abyss with a burst of bright colors.

"Mack!"

"Yes! Oh, yes, Heather."

They stilled, savoring the last of the rippling waves that flowed through them, awed by the wonder of it all, by the very power and beauty of what they had shared.

Mack kissed Heather deeply, then moved off of her,

his energy spent. He settled next to her, ignoring the fiery pain in his shoulder. She splayed one hand on his chest, her fingers nestled in the moist, dark curls, as Mack rested his lips lightly on her dewy forehead.

"I never knew..." Heather said, then paused to take a shuddering breath. "I just didn't know it could be like that. I have never experienced anything so...so wonderful, so..." Her voice trailed off as words failed her.

"It really was...sensational," Mack said quietly, "but that's not a good enough description. All I know is that it was very special, far beyond anything I've ever...never mind. Words would diminish it some-how." He paused. "Just don't be sorry it happened. Okay?"

"No regrets, Mack. I promised you that and I meant it. Mmm. I'm so sleepy."

"Then sleep, Cinderella," he said. "I'll leave in a little while and I'll try not to wake you when I go. If I'm still here in the morning, the whole neighborhood would know about it in about five seconds."

"That's true," Heather said. "If it wasn't for the twins, I'd say let the neighbors enjoy the gossip, but it wouldn't be fair to the girls, plus I don't want to have to answer the questions they would most defi-nitely ask."

Mack chuckled. "Oh, yes, most definitely. How's this? I'll come back in the morning, wearing different clothes, you understand, and bring breakfast for us all. Something like strawberries and bagels."

"Nice," Heather said, then yawned. "Mmm."

Heather drifted off to sleep and Mack sifted his fingers through her silky hair. As he gazed at her lovely, peaceful face, he allowed himself to relive what they had just shared, knowing he would, indeed, cherish the memories of this night and all that had taken place between them.

He frowned in the next instant as Heather's words began to whisper in his mind, then gain volume.

No past. No future. Just now.

Well, yeah, he thought, that was fine, exactly right. The lovemaking they'd shared had been mutually agreed upon, no strings attached, no demands for a commitment hovering in the shadows waiting to pounce.

It had nothing to do with their pasts, certainly didn't change the future that had him leaving Tucson in a little more than a week. It had been in the now, just as Heather had said. The perfect ending to a fairy-tale night. Yes, what Heather had said earlier was right on the money. No past. No future. Just now.

Then why, Mack asked himself, did the echo of those words disturb him, cause a chill to sweep through him and replace the pleasant warmth of being physically sated? This didn't make sense, not one bit.

"Damn," he muttered. Those words were going to ruin this night for him if they didn't go away and leave him alone.

Mack rotated his shoulder in an attempt to relieve some of the throbbing pain, then sighed. He'd better leave, he thought. He might fall asleep and blow the whole thing by still being there in the morning. No, he probably wouldn't be able to sleep without taking something for the pain in his shoulder.

Maybe if he left Heather, this bed, the house, he could leave her haunting words behind, wouldn't have to hear them, deal with them, wouldn't have to question why they were causing him to wish she had never said them.

Mack kissed Heather on the forehead, then eased off the bed and dressed quickly. He stood by the side of the bed and stared down at her for a long moment, filling his senses with the very sight of her. Then he turned and left the room and the house, closing the front door behind him with a quiet click.

"What did you have for dessert?" Melissa said from where she was lying on her stomach on Heather's bed. "Chocolate something?"

Emma crawled up on the bed and matched her sister's pose, the pair watching Heather braid her hair as she stood in front of the mirror on the back of the door. She was wearing jeans and a pink cotton blouse.

"No, I was too full for dessert," Heather said, "because I ate every bite of my dinner. It was delicious."

"Tell me again about the lights you called that fancy name," Emma said.

"Chandeliers," Heather said. "They were so beautiful, like twinkling stars, or sparkling diamonds. It really was a place for a princess and I felt so pretty in my special dress. You saw Uncle Mack when he came to pick me up. He was so handsome in his suit, just like Prince Charming was for Cinderella.''

"Wow," Emma said. "Cinderella and Prince Charming and stuff."

"Did you lose one of your shoes?" Melissa said.

Heather laughed. "No, I didn't need to. Uncle Mack knows who I am and where I am. He doesn't have to travel all over the kingdom to find the princess the shoe fits. In fact, he'll be here in a bit because he said he'd bring us a fun breakfast. How's that?"

"Cool," Melissa said.

"What did you do when you came home?" Emma said. "Watch TV? We saw a video about a zillion Dalmatian puppies at Becky's and ate tons of popcorn. It was fun. What did you and Uncle Mack do?"

A warm flush crept up Heather's cheeks. "Where did I put that rubber band for my braid?"

"It's on the top of the dresser," Emma said.

"Oh, so it is," Heather said. "Do you two want to go out front and wait for Uncle Mack? I'll set the table for breakfast."

"'Kay," the girls said in unison, then slid off the bed and ran from the room.

Heather wrapped the rubber band around the end of her braid, then leaned forward and gazed at her reflection in the mirror.

"What did you do when you and Uncle Mack came home, Ms. Marshall?" she said, unable to curb the smile that appeared on her lips. "Oh, my, it was so wonderful, so…"

Heather moved to the bed, sat on the edge, than ran her hand slowly over the spread, the memories of the previous night filling her heart and mind with vivid and exquisite images.

So wrong? she asked herself, her smile changing into a frown. No, she wasn't going to even entertain the idea that she'd made a dangerous, emotional mistake by making love with Mack.

While she was a bit shocked at her own boldness, announcing to the man that she wanted to make love with him, she did *not* regret what had happened between them.

And taking that momentous step with Mack was not going to result in her being hurt in any way. When Mack left Tucson, he would not take her memories, nor her heart with him.

Well, sure, she would miss Mack, just as Melissa and Emma would, might even get misty when the final goodbyes were exchanged, but she wasn't going to ache with that missing, be consumed with loneliness. She wouldn't cry through the dark hours of the night. Nope. Wouldn't happen.

"I'm all grown up, so worldly and sophisticated," Heather said, laughing as she got to her feet. "Ta-da. This is the new me."

Humming a peppy tune, she left the bedroom and went to the kitchen where she set the table for breakfast. She made a pot of coffee and a pitcher of orange juice, then glanced at her watch.

Mack would probably arrive at any moment, she thought, with a delectable breakfast in tow, and she was definitely hungry.

Mack, she mused, leaning back against the counter and staring into space. What was *he* thinking on this morning after? Did *he* regret what had happened between them? Oh, what a gloomy idea. No, she doubted that he had any misgivings about their lovemaking. He was very experienced in this type of thing. If *she* was comfortable with what had transpired, then Mack certainly was, too. Fine. No problem.

So, bring on the strawberries and bagels, Mr. Marshall, it's time for the morning meal around here. The girls had never had bagels. And if they stayed true to form, they'd love them for the simple reason that their uncle Mack had brought them and, heaven knew, he wouldn't ask them to eat anything yucky or—

"Mom!" Emma yelled, running into the house and bringing Heather from her rambling thoughts. "Melissa's stuck up in the tree, really high, and she can't get down, and she's crying, and she was trying to save a kitty that was up there, and...you gotta get her, Mom."

"Oh, dear heaven," Heather said, rushing from the kitchen.

Heather dashed out the front door with Melissa right behind her and saw Mack standing beneath the tall mulberry tree in the front yard. Her breath caught as she stopped by his side and looked up into the thick branches of the tree, Melissa far above her.

"Don't move, Melissa," Mack said. "Just stay very still until we figure out how to get you down."

"I'm scared, Uncle Mack," Melissa said, sobbing. "Mommy, I want to get down from here."

"We'll get you, I promise, Melissa," Heather said. "But, please, stay very still for now. Will you do that, sweetheart?"

"'Kay," Melissa said, then sniffled.

"Do you have a ladder?" Mack said to Heather.

"No, but Susie does," Heather said, her voice trembling. "I'll go get it right now. Keep talking to Melissa, Mack, tell her over and over not to move or...oh, God, she's so far up there."

Mack gripped Heather's shoulders.

"Stay calm," he said. "If Melissa realizes how upset you are, she'll become even more frightened."

"Yes. Yes, you're right," Heather said, nodding jerkily. "I'm okay. I'll...I'll go get the ladder."

"Good, that's good." Mack brushed his lips over hers. "Go."

Heather turned and ran down the block as fast as she could, fear for her daughter consuming her, causing her to stumble, then regain her balance. At Susie's, Heather pounded on the door, calling her friend's name. Susie flung open the door a second later.

Feeling as though she was moving in agonizingly slow motion, Heather helped Susie to retrieve a ladder from a shed at the end of Susie's narrow driveway, then with Buzzy running on ahead, the two mothers carried the ladder back to the mulberry tree. Other neighbors began to appear as they heard the commotion and made their way quickly toward the Marshalls' house.

When Heather and Susie were within fifteen feet of the yard, Emma shrieked in terror as Melissa lost her footing on the branch where she was perched and screamed as she began to fall.

"No!" Heather yelled, dropping her end of the ladder. "Melissa!" She ran, the distance to her falling child seeming like miles. "No!"

As Melissa crashed through the last branches on the tree, Mack extended his arms and caught her, the impact causing him to lose his balance. He spun around as he felt himself falling, then landed on his back on the hard ground with Melissa held tightly against his chest.

Heather dropped to her knees beside the pair and Melissa flung herself at her mother, wrapping her arms around Heather's neck and crying.

Mack sat up and draped his arms over his bent knees, sucking in deep breaths.

A cheer went up from the assembled group, then voices buzzed as everyone talked at once, exclaiming over Mack's heroic rescue.

"You're all right. You're all right," Heather said, struggling against threatening tears as she rubbed Melissa's back. "Uncle Mack saved you and you're fine. You're just scratched up a little, but Mommy will fix those cuts and you can have lots of bandages. Shh, don't cry, sweetheart. You're safe now. Can you stop crying now, Melissa, so we can thank Uncle Mack for keeping you from being terribly hurt? Don't you think it's time to say thank-you?''

Melissa nodded, sniffled, then eased out of Heather's embrace to stand next to her mother, who was still kneeling on the ground. The pair turned to look at Mack where he sat on the ground, his chin lowered to his chest.

''Mack?'' Heather said.

Mack raised his head slowly to look at Heather, straightening his shoulders slightly in the process.

''Melissa and I are so grateful to you for...'' Heather started, then her eyes widened and her heart began to race. ''Oh, dear God. Mack, your shirt...your shoulder...you're bleeding. Oh, God, Mack?''

A stunned hush fell over the neighbors, except for Melissa and Emma, who burst into tears again when they saw the blood spreading on Mack's dusty, white shirt.

Mack took a ragged breath, then attempted and failed to produce a smile.

''Houston,'' he said, his voice strained by pain, ''we have a problem.''

Chapter Eleven

Heather sat in the crowded waiting room at the hospital, her hands clutched tightly in her lap. She looked up at the clock on the wall, then shook her head in self-disgust as she realized it had only been two minutes since she'd last checked to see how much time had passed since Mack was whisked away down a corridor. She leaned her head back against the wall and closed her eyes.

What a nightmare. She should be counting her blessings, she knew, that Melissa had not been seriously injured when she'd fallen through the branches of the tree. Yes, Melissa was fine, but Mack was not and it was terrifying.

There had been so much blood on Mack's shirt, and

the ugly red stain had continued to spread during the trip to the hospital. Mack had been pale and hadn't spoken, his jaw clenched from pain as she'd driven above the speed limit across town.

The wound on Mack's shoulder had been obviously torn open from the impact of catching Melissa. Mack had saved her daughter from being terribly injured, maybe even killed, but at what cost to himself? There had been so much blood on his shirt and—

Oh, God, she hated this. She couldn't bear the thought of Mack going through heaven-only-knew-what down that ominous hallway, so far away, with no one telling her a single thing about his condition. What if the reopening of his wound resulted in permanent damage to his shoulder, the range of movement of his arm, or—

"Marshall?" a man said from the doorway of the waiting room. He was wearing green scrubs that were splattered with blood.

Heather jumped to her feet. "Yes. I'm Heather Marshall."

"Would you come with me, please, Mrs. Marshall?" the man said. "I'd like to explain your husband's condition before you see him."

"Oh, he's not..." Heather started, then stopped speaking as she hurried across the room. Shut up, Heather. She'd allow them to believe that she was Mack's wife. If they knew she wasn't, they might not tell her anything. "How is Mack?" she said when she reached the man.

"I'm Dr. Kildare," the man said, smiling. "Yep, that's really my name. I wanted to be a firefighter when I grew up, but..." He shrugged. "With a last name like Kildare what choice did I have but to become a doctor? Let's go into one of the empty rooms so we can talk, shall we?"

"Yes, yes, of course," Heather said, managing to produce a weak smile as she realized the doctor was attempting to relieve some of her stress with his banter. "I'm sure Mack is doing fine if he's in the hands of Dr. Kildare. Right? Oh, please, tell me I'm right."

The doctor escorted Heather into an empty examining room, waved her onto a chair, then pulled another chair in front of her and sat.

"Okay," he said, "here's the scoop. Your husband tore open the wound in his shoulder when he caught the fearless Melissa when she fell out of the tree. How did the kitten make out?"

"The kitten?" Heather said, staring at him blankly. "Oh, the kitten. Well, I vaguely recall that Emma, Melissa's twin sister, was carrying the kitten when my neighbor, Susie, hustled them down the block to...why are we talking about that cat?"

"Because you're the color of paste," Dr. Kildare said, "and I'm chatting with you a bit here to see if you're going to blink out on me. Why don't you take a nice deep breath, and let it out slowly, very slowly."

Heather did as instructed, then lifted her chin. "Thank you. I'm fine now. How's Mack?"

"In a world of hurt at the moment," the doctor said.

"I cleaned up the wound and restitched it. Then I telephoned the doctor in New York City who has been treating your husband's injury. We agreed on a course of treatment."

Heather nodded, her gaze riveted on the doctor.

"I've got Mack wrapped like a mummy," the doctor went on, "to keep his arm completely immobile until those stitches can take hold. He's not to use that arm for anything. I'll give you a plastic covering so he can take a shower, but he'll have to have help cutting his meat, tying his shoes, doing whatever takes two hands to do.

"He needs to rest, too, so I've told him to take the pain pills I'll be sending along. His body needs time to recuperate from the trauma, and it's not going to do that if he's rockin' and rollin'. Sit on his chest if you have to, but he's to stay put."

"I understand," Heather said.

"Good," Dr. Kildare said. "I gave him a whopping big shot of painkiller so he ought to be pretty spacey by now. Take him home and put him to bed. Bring him back here in a week so I can see how we're doing. Any questions?"

"No. No, I don't think so."

Dr. Kildare got to his feet. "We tossed his shirt, so I cut a scrub top down the front and draped it around him. He's a real fashion statement. Okay, let's go collect the hero and you can get out of here."

Heather followed the doctor from the room and farther down the hall to another one, very aware that her legs were trembling and her heart was thudding wildly.

"Okay, hotshot," the doctor said, entering the room with Heather right behind him, "your wife is in charge and you're to follow her orders to the letter."

Mack blinked, shook his head slightly, then rose slowly from the chair he was sitting on.

"My who?" he said, his voice rather thick.

"Me. Honey." Heather went to Mack's side and gripped his right arm. "Your wife? Heather? Remember? The person the doctor is releasing you to, because if you didn't have me, your loving wife, they'd probably insist on keeping you here in the hospital? Are you with me?"

"Got it," Mack said, then weaved unsteadily on his feet. "Honey."

"I'll get an orderly with a wheelchair," Dr. Kildare said. "Sit back down, big guy, before you fall on your face."

"You bet," Mack said, thudding onto the chair as the doctor strode from the room. "Honey."

"No. *I'm* honey," Heather said. "He's Dr. Kildare. Oh, never mind. Mack, I'm so sorry this happened. I'll be forever grateful for what you did for Melissa, but...I'm just so sorry about your shoulder and—"

"Doesn't matter as long as Melissa is okay." Mack stared into space. "What happened to the strawberries and bagels?"

"Huh?" Heather said, frowning. "Oh, the breakfast you brought to the house. I don't know what...yes, I do. You must have set the grocery sack on the sidewalk when you saw what was happening to Melissa.

"Susie snatched up the sack with the promise of a yummy breakfast for the twins and Buzzy as she herded them off. She was trying to get the girls to stop crying. They were very upset when they saw all that blood on your shirt. Susie is going to tend to Melissa's scratches and..."

Heather giggled, the sound slightly hysterical. "Emma was carrying the kitten who started this whole nightmare, although I have no idea how the dumb thing got out of the tree. There. That covers it."

"Except there's something I've been wondering about," Mack said, his speech becoming more slurred by the moment. "Why did Susie name her son Buzzy?"

"I don't believe this," Heather said, rolling her eyes heavenward. "Susie named him Donald when he was born. The Buzzy business started when he was about four and insisted on having a buzz cut, because his hair was naturally curly and he hated it, and he intends to go through life looking like he's in boot camp and...oh, Mack..."

"Hmm?" he said, then blinked slowly.

Heather sniffled. "I was so scared when I saw the blood on your shirt. I don't want you to be hurt. I'm so sorry this happened."

Mack reached out to pat Heather on the arm but missed. "I'm fine," he said. "Perfectly fine. Never been better. Don't be upset. Honey. Let it not be said that Mack Marshall caused his beloved wife to be upset. No, sir, not me. Susie ripped off my strawberries and bagels, but I ended up with a wife. Pretty good trade-off, wouldn't you say? Yeppa. Just dandy. Let's make a baby. Maybe you'll have twins again, lovely wife. That would be fun.''

''Mack, hush,'' Heather said, feeling a warm flush on her cheeks.

An orderly entered the room, pushing a wheelchair. ''Hi, folks,'' he said. ''Your taxi is here.''

''My wife, my honey and I are going to have a baby,'' Mack said, his eyes at half-mast. ''Twins maybe. Oh, and we're going to get a dog and name him Butch.''

''Well, that's nice news,'' the orderly said. ''Congratulations.''

''He's a tad…under the weather,'' Heather said. ''We're not really having twins. What I mean is…oh, for Pete's sake, this is insane. I'll go move my car to the front entrance.''

''I'll meet you there,'' the orderly said. ''You're only pregnant with one baby? That's too bad. Twins are really cute when you see them in one of those fancy strollers in the grocery store and—''

''I'm getting the car. Right now,'' Heather said, then nearly ran from the room.

Almost two hours later Heather took a bite of a sandwich she had no appetite for, chewed, swallowed, then sighed as she plopped the sandwich back onto the plate.

"Oh, no, you don't," Susie said, sitting opposite Heather at the Marshalls' kitchen table. "Eat every bit of that thing. You've been running on high-octane adrenaline and you have to replenish your protein grams, or some such thing."

Heather nodded and took another nibble.

"I just peeked in on Mack," Susie said. "Good grief, that man is gorgeous. Anyway, he's sleeping like a baby in your bed, and I had to hold myself back to keep from crawling in next to him. Not that he'd know that I was there. He's out cold."

"They gave him a big shot of painkiller at the hospital." Heather paused. "I wish I could have seen Melissa before you took the kids to the movies. You're sure she's all right?"

"Trust me, Heather, she's fine. She's retelling her adventure ad nauseam and every time she does she's higher in the tree. She's got a zillion Rugrats bandages on her cute little body and is strutting her stuff.

"I assured Buzzy and the twins that Mack would be just fine, snatched up Becky to baby-sit the crew at the movies and that is that. I figured that you and Mack didn't need the kids hovering around when you brought him home. I also didn't know what condition he would be in. There sure was a gruesome amount of blood on his shirt when you left here to go to the hospital."

"I know," Heather said quietly. "It was terrifying.

Once I knew that Melissa was all right and focused on Mack, I was so upset, so…'' She shook her head as threatening tears closed her throat.

''You really care for Mack, don't you?'' Susie said. ''No, wait a minute. Don't give me a spiel about him being a member of the family. I'm not buying that. I'm talking about a woman having feelings for a special man in her life.''

''Don't be silly,'' Heather said, poking a hole in her sandwich.

''Eat it, don't kill it,'' Susie said. ''I'm not being silly, Heather Marshall. I witnessed the look on your face when you saw that blood on Mack's shirt. That was not the twins' mother being concerned about dear ole Uncle Mack. That was one hundred-percent-woman coming unglued because her man was hurt.''

''No, I…'' Heather started, then stopped speaking for a moment. ''Yes, all right, I care for Mack. A lot. As a woman.''

Susie leaned forward. ''How much is a lot?''

''More than a little.''

''Now we're getting somewhere,'' Susie said, rubbing her hands together. ''Did you make love with him when you came home from your big dinner date last night? Emma told me all about your princess dress and the fancy restaurant Mack took you to. So? Did you two do the deed?''

''Susie, for heaven's sake,'' Heather said, feeling a warm flush on her cheeks.

''Eureka! You're blushing. You did it. The big

'it.'" Susie smiled in delight. "That is fantastic. You are so overdue for some 'it,' it's a crime. I know you, Heather. You wouldn't have slept with the man if your feelings didn't run deep, very deep, for him. So? Where do you and Mack go from here?"

"Nowhere, Susie," Heather said, pushing the plate with the punctured sandwich to one side. "Mack is leaving to return to New York a week from Monday and..." She paused. "Well, maybe not. That could be postponed a tad, depending on how his shoulder is doing, I guess. But that's beside the point. The fact remains that he *will* be leaving. End of story."

"Why?"

"Why what?" Heather said, frowning in confusion.

"Why is it the end of the story? Come on, Heather, get real. Mack could have established his role as uncle to the girls days ago and been out of here. I firmly believe that he's been hanging around to be close to you, too. I'd bet a buck that he cares *a lot* for you, just as you do for him. From where I'm sitting, this story is just beginning, not ending."

"You don't understand," Heather said.

"So clue me in."

"Susie, Mack has made it perfectly clear to me and to the twins that he is not the kind of man who puts down roots. He has to be free in order to be happy, who he is. Mack and I are as different as day and night, totally incompatible."

"I'm guessing there's one arena where you're *very* compatible," Susie said, smiling and wiggling her eyebrows. "Oh, how cute. I made you blush again. You're the only person I know who still blushes."

"Would you cut that out?" Heather said. "Listen to me for a minute."

"I'm all ears."

"Okay. Reality-check time. Mack must be footloose and fancy free to be content. Me? I have no intention of becoming involved in a serious relationship with him, or any man for that matter, because I've had more than enough heartache from loving and losing. I won't do it. I won't.

"I gave myself a night of being Cinderella with her Prince Charming. It was a gift, a precious gift, and I'll cherish the memories. But that's all there is…just memories. Mack will leave. I'll continue on as I've been. And someday the girls and I will achieve our dream of having our own home. Nothing in that future I'm describing includes Mack Marshall, except for maybe a Christmas card from him."

"Oh-h-h, that is the saddest thing I've ever heard." Susie smacked the table with the palm of one hand, causing Heather to jerk in her chair. "No, I won't accept that. It's too cold, empty, lonely and grim. People can change, Heather. Mack could learn to stay put. You could learn to let go of your ghosts from the past. The two of you could—"

"No!" Heather interrupted. "I'm being very realistic about this and the subject is closed."

"You're a dud," Susie said, glaring at her.

"So be it," Heather said, lifting her chin.

"What about the fact that Mack is camped out in your bed? Huh? Answer me that."

"Well, it's the least I can do, considering the fact he saved my child's life, or if not that, he certainly kept Melissa from being seriously injured. I'll sleep on the sofa while Mack is recuperating. I'll cook his meals, cut his meat, do whatever he needs while he can't use his arm. Then later...he'll...later he'll leave as...planned and that will...be fine and...well, sure I'll miss him for a while but that's only natural because...because..."

"Because you're falling in love with him," Susie said decisively.

"I'm ignoring you, Susie Jenkins," Heather said. "How much do I owe you for the girls' movie tickets and my share of hiring Becky to watch over them?"

"It's my treat. It's not every day of the week that I get strawberries and bagels for breakfast. I came out the winner in this deal." Susie paused. "Listen, why don't you stretch out on the sofa and take a nap while the kids are gone. You've got to be emotionally and physically drained from this morning's fun and games. I'll pick up the kids later, so don't worry about that."

"Thank you for everything, Susie," Heather said. "You've been wonderful through this nightmare, just stepped in and took charge and I appreciate it so much."

"That's what friends are for," she said, getting to her feet. "Friends also have the privilege of telling it like it is. I sincerely believe you're falling in love with

Mack, Heather, and that you're being too quick to whip out the end-of-the-story bit. Oh, by the way, you now own a baby girl kitten. Emma smuggled it into the movies under her shirt and has named it Maxine in honor of her uncle Mack, who saved her very own kitten's life, as well as her twin sister's.''

"Oh, good night," Heather said, rolling her eyes heavenward. "That's all we need around here... another mouth to feed."

"Hey, look at the bright side," Susie said, starting across the room. "It could have been a pit bull that Melissa had been determined to go after in that tree. Emma would be trying to smuggle *that* beast into the movies."

Heather laughed. "Perish the thought. Emma is really attached to this kitty already?"

"Like super glue," Susie said as she left the kitchen. "Maxine is a Marshall, no doubt about it. See you later, Heather."

"Thanks again, Susie," Heather called after her.

After Susie left, a silence fell over the kitchen and with it came a wave of exhaustion that swept through Heather. She got to her feet, her destination the lumpy sofa in the living room where, she decided, she would indulge in a short nap. When she reached the sofa, she hesitated, glancing in the direction of the hall leading to her bedroom.

She'd check on Mack before she allowed herself to collapse and rest, she thought, make certain that he was still soundly asleep and didn't need anything.

In her bedroom, Heather placed her computer chair next to the bed and sat, her gaze riveted on Mack who was deeply asleep.

He was pale beneath his tan, and the bulky white bandage that encased his shoulder, arm and chest looked heavy and uncomfortable.

Oh, Mack, I'm so sorry this happened, Heather thought, tears misting her eyes. She wished she could turn back the clock to before she had told the twins to go outside and wait for their uncle Mack, had asked them, instead, to help her set the table for breakfast.

She'd shooed the girls from her bedroom because they were pressing her about what she and Uncle Mack had done after returning to the house from the fancy restaurant the night before. To wiggle her way out of the conversation, she'd sent them to the front yard to wait for Mack.

How far back would she turn that clock if she had the magic power to do it? Would she not have made glorious love with Mack so there would be no need to avoid the topic of what had transpired when they'd returned to the house after dinner?

"No," she whispered.

Even if she had a magic wand, she wouldn't erase what she and Mack had shared last night. She intended to cherish every wondrous moment, every memory, of that beautiful joining.

Mack stirred in his sleep, groaned, then stilled.

He was in so much pain, Heather thought, fresh tears filling her eyes. She hated this, she really did.

She felt so helpless to relieve Mack's suffering. She really, *really* hated this, because she cared so much for Mack and—

The conversation with Susie suddenly floated through Heather's exhausted mind and she frowned. Susie was convinced that she was falling in love with Mack Marshall, which simply wasn't true. Susie was fantasizing, creating a romantic scenario of the young widow with the two little children finding new and lasting love and...well, it would make a good movie, but it wasn't remotely close to reality.

Yes, she cared for Mack. A lot. Which was more than a little. But that was a long way from being in the process of falling in love with the man. Nor was Mack falling in love with her.

And that was that.

And that was fine.

The way it should be, given the circumstances.

"Right, Mack?" Heather said. "Right."

Mack shifted his head on the pillow and Heather held her breath for a moment, afraid she'd disturbed him by speaking out loud. He quieted again and she got to her feet.

"Nap," she said. "I need a nap."

"Heather," Mack said, his voice thick.

Heather's eyes widened as she looked down at him, then realized he was apparently having a drug-induced dream.

"Heather," Mack said again.

Heather moved closer to the bed and leaned over. "Yes? I'm here, Mack. Just rest, sleep."

"Don't want…" he mumbled. "No."

"What don't you want?" Heather said. "Maybe I can fix it if you tell me. Oh, Mack, I don't even know if you can hear me."

Mack took a shuddering breath, but didn't open his eyes. Beads of sweat dotted his brow and Heather's heart ached as she looked at him.

"No," he repeated. "No, I don't want…don't want…to leave you, Heather. Tree roots…stay with…Heather, twins…find…my…dream…no, no… can't do it…can't do it…father's son…must go… go…go…"

Heather straightened and two tears spilled onto her cheeks.

"I know," she said, a sob catching in her throat. "I know you can't stay with me and the girls. I know that, but…"

Heather shook her head, then turned and ran from the room, tears streaming down her face.

Chapter Twelve

Mack stirred, opened his eyes slowly, then snapped them closed again as he came to the instant conclusion that there was a jackhammer pounding in his head and someone was drilling deep for oil in his shoulder. He also registered the late-arriving fact that he had absolutely no idea where he was.

"Uncle Mack?" a little voice whispered. "I saw you open your eyes. Are you awake? It's me…Melissa."

Oh, right, Mack thought groggily. Melissa, Emma…and this was Heather's bed he was occupying. Weird. He couldn't for the life of him remember how he got here.

The last clear image he had in his brain was taking

part in a rather confusing conversation with Heather in an examining room at the hospital. Beyond that…nothing; his mind was a total blank.

"Uncle Mack?"

Mack opened his eyes again and turned his throbbing head on the pillow to see Melissa standing next to the bed. She was wearing her nightgown and had bandages on her forehead and chin with cartoon pictures of a strange-looking bald kid, and another one with orange hair, buck teeth and heavy square glasses.

"Hi, Melissa," he said. "How ya doin'? Cool bandages you've got there."

"Rugrats," Melissa said, her voice still very hushed. "I snuck in here to see you while my mom is on the phone, 'cause I gotta talk to you, I really do."

Mack shifted slightly and stifled a groan as the pain in his shoulder increased, shooting all the way down to the tips of his fingers.

"Go for it," he said. "What's on your mind?"

Melissa glanced quickly at the door, then leaned closer to Mack, her nose only inches from his.

"I wanna say thank you a bunch for catching me when I fell out of the tree 'cause I really didn't want to die and go to heaven and be an angel yet, and I'm really, really sorry that your shoulder got all icky and bloody and stuff 'cause you grabbed me 'fore I splatted on the ground, and…and…" Tears filled Melissa's eyes. "And I love you, Uncle Mack, and I hope you feel better real soon."

"Ah, Melissa," Mack said, a strange achy sensation gripping his throat as she finished speaking her heartfelt words. "I'm going to be just fine. Don't you worry about that. I'm just glad you're all right, sweetheart. Hey, I'm going to complain to the doctor about this boring white bandage he has me wrapped in. He didn't even give me cool stuff like Rugrats."

Melissa frowned. "Buzzy's mom used up all their Rugrats bandages on me. Maybe I can take some pennies out of the dream piggy and buy you some."

"No, no," Mack said quickly. "Those pennies are for your very own home, your dream. You can't use them for anything else. I really don't need Rugrats bandages. Okay?"

"'Kay...I guess." Melissa sniffled. "Are you sure the doctor fixed you good? I don't want you to die and go to heaven and be an angel, either."

Mack chuckled. "I don't think I'm a candidate for being an angel. The image doesn't quite fit. Anyway, I promise you that I'm going to be all right. I just need a little bit of time for my shoulder to heal up again."

"That's good," Melissa said, nodding. "That's really good. You can stay right there in Mommy's bed and heal up like you said."

"Well, that's a nice offer," Mack said, "but I'll be heading back to my hotel in the morning."

"Wrong," Heather said, coming into the room. "You're not going anywhere, Mr. Marshall. Melissa, what are you doing in here? I told you that Uncle Mack had to get his rest."

"He opened his eyes, Mom," Melissa said. "I stood here, and stood here, and then he opened his eyes. I had to tell him I'm glad he caught me when I fell out of the tree 'cause I don't want to be an angel in heaven yet."

"I see," Heather said, smiling warmly at her daughter. "Well, I'm glad you realized that you owed Uncle Mack a big thank-you. Go have your snack with Emma, then it will be time for bed."

"'Kay." Melissa kissed Mack on the cheek, then hiked up her nightgown and ran from the room.

Heather sat in the chair next to the bed.

"You slept for hours, Mack," she said. "Dr. Kildare wasn't kidding when he said he'd given you a whopping big pain shot."

"Dr. Kildare?"

"That was his name. Don't you remember?"

"Vaguely," Mack said. "The scene at the hospital is sort of a blur in my mind. I seem to recall a conversation that didn't make much sense."

"Oh, *that,*" Heather said, smiling. "You're probably getting flashes of when I was passing myself off as your wife because I was afraid they wouldn't tell me anything about your condition if I didn't, might have even insisted on keeping you there."

"Oh, yeah," Mack said. "Honey." He paused. "Hey, look at that. You're blushing."

"You and Susie should start a club."

"Huh?"

"Never mind," Heather said, shaking her head.

"How are you feeling? Do you think you could eat something?"

"I feel like I've been run over by a very large truck," Mack said, "and thank you but no, I'm not hungry."

"Well, in the morning you're going to have to eat, hungry or not. Your body needs nourishment in order to heal properly."

"Yes, ma'am," he said. "When I get back to the hotel tomorrow, I'll have room service bring me one of everything on the menu. How's that?"

"*That* is not going to happen because you're staying right where you are," Heather said. "You heard me say that while Melissa was still here in the room. This isn't open for discussion, Mack. The doctor was very adamant about the importance of your getting the proper rest you need and having help doing things that take two hands to accomplish. Consider yourself a prisoner in my bed."

"I'd have to be a fool to complain about that." Mack smiled. "Gotcha. You're blushing again." His smiled faded. "We never got a chance to do the…you know…the morning-after thing. No regrets?"

"None. I promised you that," she said. "It was a beautiful, memory-making night."

No past. No future. Just now.

There were those words again, hollering like crazy in his head. The words that caused a cold fist to tighten in his gut, and threw him off-kilter. Which didn't make a damn bit of sense. Forget it, he told himself. He didn't have the energy to explore his feelings at the moment.

"Heather," he said, "I really can't stay here. You have enough to do with it being tax season without playing nursemaid to me."

"Are you thirsty?"

"You are *not* listening to me, Heather," Mack said, frowning.

"Nope, I'm not," Heather said, getting to her feet and starting across the room. "You're just going to have to live with the fact that you're going to be the recipient of some good old-fashioned tender lovin' care, Marshall style." She stopped at the doorway and glanced back at Mack over her shoulder. "Honey."

Mack chuckled as Heather disappeared from his view.

Honey, his mind echoed. Yes, it was all coming back to him now, the scene in the examining room. Heather had been fantastic, so quick on her feet, just stepped up and declared herself to be his wife.

He could remember too that in his very drugged state he'd liked the sound of it all…he and Heather as husband and wife, having pledged their love and exchanged vows declaring they would be together forever. He'd even told her that they should make a baby, might even create cute little twins.

Man, a hefty serving of potent drugs sure could scramble a person's brain. Mack Marshall married? Mack Marshall so deeply in love that he intended to spend the remainder of his days with Heather, as her husband, the father of Melissa and Emma? Hoped to be blessed with more babies born of his love for Heather? To settle in and settle down in one spot? Have roots like a tree?

"Never happen," he muttered, then moved carefully to attempt to ease the pain in his shoulder.

Would it?

No, no, of course not. But why, he wondered, was he registering such a sense of relief and well-being, knowing he was going to be staying right where he was until his shoulder was on the mend?

The image of his big, fancy hotel suite was so cold, empty and lonely. But here? In this shabby little house? There was warmth and laughter here, sunshine and caring, and...and love? Not just family love, not just Uncle Mack love, but man and woman love, Mack and Heather love? *In* love? With each other?

Ah, come on, Marshall, get a grip. He was still under the influence of the drugs, wasn't thinking straight. He wasn't falling in love with Heather.

Just because he couldn't bear the thought of leaving her, just because the lovemaking he'd shared with her had been not only physically sensational but had evoked emotions he'd never felt before, just because his heart quickened at the very sight of Heather Marshall didn't mean...

"Oh-h-h, cripe," he said, dragging his free hand down his face.

His agent, Marilyn, who had known him for more years than he could count, had told him days ago that he had "heart trouble" in regard to Heather. Mack Marshall, she had said, was down for the count.

He'd chalked up the malarkey she was laying on him to the fact that he had wakened her in the middle of the night.

But what had prompted Marilyn to say all that? What had he said and how had he said it that had caused her to reach such a far-out conclusion?

Oh, forget this nonsense. If a man was in love with a woman, he sure as hell would know it. Wouldn't he? But what if that man had never been in love, didn't know what the signs and signals were? Could love sneak up on a guy and knock him over without him even being aware that it was happening? Damn it, he didn't know the answer to that question. He didn't know, at the moment, a helluva lot of things.

Well, he'd better figure out what was going on because this was going to drive him right out of his mind. But then again, even if he *was* in love with Heather, it wouldn't change the ultimate outcome. He was still his father's son, had to be on the move, couldn't be a tree with roots. So why bother to attempt to discover his true feelings for Heather? He'd be leaving Tucson just as soon as he was able to travel and—

And he didn't want to go!

"That's it," Mack said. "That's all. I refuse to carry on any further nonsensical conversations with myself. Brain, turn off. I'm going to sleep."

Mack closed his eyes and willed himself to relax,

to let the silence of sleep claim him, to gain a reprieve from his tangled thoughts.

''Mack?''

He opened his eyes again and drank in the sight of the trio standing at the foot of the bed. The twins were standing on either side of Heather in their matching nightgowns and Heather had her arms wrapped around each of her beautiful daughters.

There they were, he thought, his heart racing. Heather, Melissa and Emma. His family. There they were. The ones who would cry if he died. There they were. The mother, the children, who were so real and honest and wonderful, and who had accepted him unconditionally, welcomed him, made room for him in their lives.

And there *she* was.

Heather.

The woman.

The woman who had stolen his heart for all time.

The woman, he suddenly knew without a single doubt, whom he loved with every breath in his battered body.

The woman he was going to leave without her ever knowing how he felt because he couldn't be for her what she deserved to have.

And, oh, how it hurt, the pain far greater than the discomfort from his demolished shoulder. Yes, he'd spend the rest of his life alone as he'd always been, but now, because of loving Heather, he'd spend the rest of his life…lonely.

"Mack, the girls would like to say good-night to you," Heather said.

"Sure," he said, hearing the raspy edge in his voice as emotions swamped him. "You bet."

Melissa and Emma came around to the side of the bed, then took turns kissing him on the cheek.

"Good night, Uncle Mack," they said in unison.

Good night, Daddy, Mack's mind taunted.

"Sleep well," he said, his voice a hoarse whisper.

"I'll tuck them in, hear their prayers, then be back to check on you, Mack," Heather said. "Maybe you'll reconsider eating something. Come on, sweeties, off to bed with you."

Mustering every ounce of willpower he possessed, Mack forced his mind to become blank, allowed no further thoughts to surface. When Heather returned and sat in the chair next to the bed, he stared straight ahead, not looking at her.

"Would you try to eat something?" she said.

"No. Thank you." Mack paused. "Where are you going to sleep?"

"On the sofa in the living room."

Mack continued to look at a spot on the far wall. "Your sofa is lumpy, Heather. You won't rest well there. I'm feeling very guilty about taking your bed."

"Don't be silly," she said. "The sofa will be fine. I'm more concerned about having to work in here, continually disturbing you when you should be resting."

"You won't disturb me. The hum of a computer

and the clicking of keys isn't exactly sonic-boom-level noise. Besides, I'll be up and around tomorrow.''

"We'll see about that." Heather leaned forward slightly. "Is there some reason why you're not looking at me, Mack?''

Oh, hell, no, he thought frantically. Only the fact that he'd just discovered he was irrevocably in love with her and had no idea if it would show somehow in his eyes, on his face.

Mack turned his head on the pillow and concentrated on the space two inches above Heather's head.

"I'm...I'm wiped out," he said. "Can't believe how tired I am, considering I slept all day. But, man, I'm beat. Need some more sleep. Yep, that's it. I'm going to sleep now. Good night, Heather. Thanks for the bed, and the tender lovin' care and the...see ya.''

Heather frowned and cocked her head to one side. "Are you all right? You're acting...I don't know...rather strangely.''

"Drug residue," he said. "That's what it is. I'll be fine in the morning. No problem.''

Heather stood, then bent over and brushed her lips over Mack's, nearly causing him to groan out loud.

"I'll just gather my nightclothes, then shut off the light and let you get to sleep," she said. "Promise me that you'll call me if you need me in the night.''

I need you for the rest of my life, Mack thought, a wave of dark despair coursing through him. *But I can't have you, Heather. Oh, God, I love you so damn much.*

"Yeah. Sure," he said. "Thanks.''

Heather nodded, collected what she needed, then started toward the doorway.

"Heather," Mack said. Don't go. Stay. Here. Close. With me. Please, Heather.

"Yes?" she said, stopping to look back at him.

"Nothing," he said.

"Well, good night, Mack," she said, then turned off the light and left the room.

"Good night...my love," he whispered into the darkness. "I've got to remember, never forget.... No past. No future. Just...now."

Heather flung back the sheet, got to her feet, then turned and smoothed the bed linens she put on the sofa. She sat back down and leaned her head on the sofa top, staring up at the ceiling. The small clock on the end table announced the dismal fact that it was 1:17 a.m. and she had yet to get any sleep.

She'd like to blame her inability to escape into blissful slumber on the lumpy sofa that was substituting as her bed, but she'd be lying to herself if she did.

No, she was awake because she couldn't shut off her mind, reliving scene after scene of all that she'd shared with Mack...including the incredibly beautiful lovemaking of the night before.

Not only were the images in her mind unbelievably vivid, so were the memories of the emotions she had experienced. Everything, from the pure joy of laughing and talking with Mack, to the icy terror when she'd seen the spreading blood on his shirt.

Heather sighed wearily, then looked in the direction of the hallway that led to where Mack was sleeping in her bed. Without realizing for a moment that she had moved, she found herself on her feet and walking toward her bedroom.

She hesitated in the doorway, then moved to the side of the bed to gaze at Mack. A small gap in the curtains on the window allowed the moonlight to stream in, casting a silvery glow over him.

A shiver coursed through her and she crossed her arms and wrapped her hands around her elbows as she continued to stare at Mack, her heart racing and tears filling her eyes.

Here in the solitude and darkness of night, she thought, there was nowhere to run, nowhere to hide from the truth. There were no little girls to demand her attention or to allow her to avoid facing what she now knew.

She was in love with Mack Marshall.

Heather pressed trembling fingertips to her lips to keep a sob from escaping.

When had it happened? she thought frantically. At what point had she lost control of her emotions and succumbed to her growing feelings for Mack? When had she foolishly sentenced herself to a lifetime of crying in the darkness for the man she loved who was far, far away? The man who had captured her heart and would take it with him when he left. The man who didn't love her in return.

She didn't know. It didn't matter. Her self-disgust

at her own weakness would not diminish if she could pinpoint the moment that she'd fallen in love with Mack. She was so furious with herself, she could just scream, which would solve nothing.

Dear heaven, what was she going to do? How was she going to get through the following days without Mack realizing how she felt about him?

If he discovered her true feelings for him, it would be the final blow to her pride, her self-respect. Silly little Heather Marshall had fallen in love with a man who would never in a million years love her in return, a man who wanted no part of forever, of commitment, of having a wife and children, roots like a tree.

No, she thought fiercely, Mack would never know that she loved him. Mack would never know that the pattern of her life was repeating itself yet again. She loved someone who was going to walk out of her life, leave her to cry in the night...alone.

Tears spilled onto Heather's cheeks and she reached out one hand, wanting to touch Mack, to feel the warmth of his skin, the strength in his magnificent body, the softness of his lips that had captured hers in kisses that caused desire to consume her instantly.

Heather snatched her hand back and hurried from the room, nearly stumbling as tears blurred her vision. In the living room she curled into a ball on the sofa, hugging the bed pillow as she tried and failed to stop crying.

No past. No future. Just now.

The words she had spoken the previous night before

she and Mack had made love echoed suddenly in her mind and Heather clung to them like a lifeline.

Just now. Just now. Just now, she thought. That was how she'd survive the days, hours, minutes, until Mack left. She'd live one second at a time, get through it, then square off against the next. She could do this. She had to.

"And then Mack will get on a plane and leave," Heather whispered. "But he'll never know that I...oh, Mack, I love you so much."

Heather buried her face in the pillow and wept, feeling as though her heart was shattering into a million pieces that she'd never be able to put back together again.

Chapter Thirteen

Mack slept until noon the next day and woke feeling amazingly better…physically. His drug-induced headache was gone and the pain in his shoulder had receded to the level of a throbbing toothache.

Mentally, emotionally, he knew, he was in rough shape. He was shaken to the core over the realization that he was deeply in love with Heather, a fact that held the promise of a bleak and lonely future.

He couldn't change his stripes, the basic makeup of who he was, couldn't erase the wanderlust spirit he'd inherited from his father. He was who he was, and that truth meant that Heather would never be his.

Well, he thought dryly, if little Emma knew what had happened to her uncle Mack's heart, mind and soul, she'd be jumping up and down with joy.

Because Mack Marshall now had a dream.

He wanted to marry Heather, to stay by her side until death parted them, to be a father to the twins and to future Marshall babies.

Oh, yeah, he had a dream, but that was all it was...a fantasy, a heartfelt yearning, that never would be his. A chubby pink china dream piggy wouldn't help him to achieve it. Nothing would.

What stood between him and his dream was himself, and he was powerless to change who he was.

Mack frowned. He was assuming a lot here, he supposed, taking too much for granted. If he was a different kind of man, Heather would quickly agree to marry him, declare her love for him, want a future with him just as he did with her. Maybe her feelings for him didn't even run that deeply. She'd bid him adieu when he left, then get back to business as usual...Mack Marshall being out of sight, out of mind.

No, he thought fiercely. He didn't believe that, not for a second. Heather cared a great deal for him, he knew she did. She might even be in love with him right now, for all he knew.

He didn't care if she *had* said "no past, no future, just now" before they'd made love, because Heather was not the type of woman who would have taken that momentous step without her heart being as willing and involved as her body.

"Ah, hell," Mack said out loud, dragging his free hand across his beard-roughened jaw.

Why was he doing this to himself? Why torture

himself with the belief that Heather would—yes, damn it, she would—agree to be his wife if he was a man who would make a decent husband? He was just pouring salt in his raw, emotional wound, and enough was enough.

Mack turned his head on the pillow and saw that his clothes, including the scrub top from the hospital, were on the chair next to the bed. There was also a plastic cape of sorts that he guessed he was supposed to use to cover his huge bandage while he showered. A note had been placed on top of the pile and he shifted closer, grabbing it with his right hand.

"'We've gone to the grocery store,'" he read out loud. "'Please be careful if you get out of bed. Back about one o'clock. Heather.'"

Mack tossed back the blanket and sheet and eased himself to a sitting position on the side of the bed, gripping his injured shoulder as he moved. He groaned out loud since there was no one to hear him when the pain kicked up a notch in disapproval.

Deciding he could pass for a hundred-year-old man, he retrieved his belongings from the chair and shuffled off to the bathroom. There he found a fresh towel and washcloth laid out for him, as well as a new disposable razor.

"Tender lovin' care, Marshall style," he said quietly, running his hand over the fluffy towel.

He had a decision to make, he thought, staring at his reflection in the mirror above the sink. He could leave Tucson as quickly as possible, put distance between himself and Heather, his dream, and attempt to get on with his life, such as it was.

Or he could drag out his stay for as long as was feasible, gather more memories of Heather and the twins and tuck them safely away.

What should he do? He didn't have a clue.

When Heather, Melissa and Emma entered the house shortly after one o'clock toting grocery sacks, they found Mack sitting on the sofa, dressed in dusty, blood-splattered slacks and the green scrub top. He was cleanly shaven and his hair was still damp. Maxine, the kitten, was curled up asleep on his right thigh.

"Mack," Heather said, stopping dead in her tracks and causing Melissa to bump into her from behind. "You're not in bed."

"No, I'm baby-sitting this kitten," he said. "The two of us are great pals already."

"Isn't she cute, Uncle Mack?" Emma said. "Her name is Maxine 'cause you saved her and she's my very own kitten. I thought she was gray, but I gave her a bath and she's white."

"Yep," he said, nodding.

"Let's get these groceries put away, girls," Heather said, ignoring the racing tempo of her heart as she averted her gaze from Mack. "Uncle Mack is probably starving. I'll make lunch."

"'Kay," the twins said, then headed toward the kitchen with their sacks.

"How...how are you feeling, Mack?" Heather said as she peered into the sack she was holding.

"Not bad, considering," he said. "Listen, Heather, I called the hotel where I was staying and talked to the manager on duty. I explained the situation and he's going to pack my stuff from my room, put the suitcases in a taxi and send it over here. I need clean clothes and...well, I can leave for the airport from here. I hope that's all right with you."

"Yes, of course," she said, still not looking at him. "I'm sure you'd like to get out of those slacks and that hospital smock. Yes, it's fine that you did that, but...but you're not planning on leaving Tucson yet, are you?"

Oh, no, Mack, please, not yet, Heather thought frantically. She didn't want to say goodbye so soon. She didn't want to cry yet, not yet. But...but maybe he *should* go, because just looking at him, seeing him there in her home, was tearing her apart. She loved him so very much.

"I haven't decided exactly what the best plan of action is regarding leaving," Mack said. Oh, man, there Heather stood a few feet away and it might as well be thousands of miles because he couldn't reach for her, touch her, kiss her, declare his love for her. "I'm mulling it over."

"Mulling. Right." Heather nodded. "I see. Well, I'll go tend to this food, then make us all some lunch and...here I go, off to the kitchen to do that. 'Bye."

Mack frowned as he watched Heather hurry across the room and disappear from his view.

Was she acting strangely? he thought. No, it was probably his imagination. Maybe he'd be able to think more clearly after he'd had some food. He was a starving man, no doubt about it.

The sandwiches that Heather prepared were delicious and Mack ate two, along with some corn chips and fresh fruit. But despite having had the much-needed nourishment he was still a muddled mess and announced that he was going to stretch out on the bed and rest.

"Will I disturb you if I work in there?" Heather said. "Susie is taking Buzzy and the girls to the park this afternoon. It's rather crowded on Sunday when the weather is this nice, but it's fun."

"I'm taking Maxine with me, Uncle Mack," Emma said, "so you won't have to baby-sit her while we're gone."

"Oh, okay, Emma," he said, smiling at her. He looked at Heather. "No, you won't disturb me, Heather, if you work on the computer." *She* disturbed him, caused his heart to ache for her, just by being Heather. "I don't plan to sleep, just rest, that's all."

"Well, then I guess we all have our afternoon planned," Heather said, forcing a lightness to her voice that she definitely didn't feel. "We'll circle back later and meet at the ranch."

"Huh?" Melissa said. "What ranch?"

Heather laughed. "It's just a saying, Melissa. We won't really meet at a ranch."

"It would be cool if we did," Melissa said. "A ranch would have horses and cows and stuff."

"And lots and lots of icky chores," Heather said, smiling at her.

"Oh," Melissa said, wrinkling her nose. "I don't think we want to use the money from our dream piggy for a house on a ranch."

"What kind of home *are* you dreaming about, ladies?" Mack said. "You've never said much about it."

"One where we can each have our own bedroom," Emma said. "I'll share my room with Maxine."

"I want a big backyard to play ball in," Melissa said. "Buzzy will come visit a whole bunch of times and we'll have fun in that yard."

"And you, Heather?" Mack said.

Heather plunked one elbow on the table and rested her chin in the palm of her hand.

"New," she said, a dreamy expression on her face. "We'll be the first family to live in it and everything will be sparkling clean, the faucets won't drip, the carpet will be stain free. Yes, a brand-new house. I don't even care if it still smells like paint. We'll plant a tree and watch it grow over the years and..." She sighed. "Someday, someday, someday we'll have our new home."

Mack nodded. "I don't doubt that for a second. Your dream will come true." And his never would, no matter how much he wanted it. "That home will be filled with love and laughter and…" He stopped speaking and cleared his throat. "Well, I'm off to stretch out on the bed. Thank you for the delicious lunch."

Mack left the kitchen and as he crossed the living room a knock sounded at the front door. Melissa whizzed past him and flung open the door.

"Delivery for Mack Marshall," a man said. "I have suitcases here and a bill for driving my taxi clear from the other side of town."

Mack tended to the business at hand and a short time later was wearing clean slacks and a dress shirt. Having changed, he lay down on Heather's bed, flung his right arm across his eyes and within minutes was asleep.

Heather entered her bedroom and turned on the computer, the girls safely on their way to the promised outing in the park with Susie. As the computer was booting up, she moved to the edge of the bed and gazed at Mack, watching the steady rise and fall of his chest.

Yes, Mack, she thought, our dream house, our brand-new home, will be filled with love and laughter, but *you* won't be there. There will be an empty space within those walls and an ache in my heart for all time. I love you so much and I wish to the heavens that I didn't.

She spun around as tears threatened and soon immersed herself in work.

"I can't do this."

Heather jerked in her chair at the sudden sound of Mack's voice, then got to her feet and rushed to the side of the bed.

"What can't you do?" she said. "How can I help you, Mack?"

"I didn't mean to say that out loud," he said, "but it's probably just as well that I did. I need to talk to you, Heather."

He eased himself up to sit on the edge of the bed and patted the space next to him. Heather sat and looked at him questioningly.

"No, I can't do this," he said quietly, looking directly into her dark eyes. "I can't stay here with you knowing that…it's ripping me up and I…ah, damn it, Heather, I love you. I've fallen in love with you and because I have I have to leave…now.

"My loving you doesn't change who I am, the kind of life I need to lead to be content. I'll never be a tree with roots.

"But I have a dream now, just as Emma wanted me to have. A dream of being your husband, the twins' father, spending the rest of my life with you and…but my dream will never come true because I am who I am. Do you understand?"

Of course she did, Heather thought. She understood what she had always known…to love was to lose, to be abandoned, left to cry in the night alone.

She got to her feet and wrapped her arms around herself, her hands gripping her elbows.

"Yes, I understand perfectly," she said, her voice trembling. "For the record, Mack, I love you, too. I do. I certainly didn't intend to fall in love with you, but..." She shrugged. "I did. Aren't we a pair? We're in love with each other and it's a terrible and heart-breaking mistake." She shrugged again. "So it goes."

"You...you love me?" he said.

"Oh, yes," she said, nodding jerkily, "but that's of little importance under the circumstances." She paused. "Well, the doctors are going to have a fit that you're taking that long plane ride, but...would you like me to call and make a reservation for you?"

"Wait just a damn minute here," Mack said, his voice rising. "We just declared our love for each other and you're hustling me onto a plane so I can get the hell out of here, out of your bed, your home, your life?"

"Do you have a better plan?" she said, matching his volume. "Want to marry me, Mack? Settle in and stay put? Become the ever-famous tree with roots that will keep you with me until death parts us? Want to do that, Mack Marshall?"

"I can't!" he yelled.

"I know! So...so go, just go and let me get on with my life." Tears filled her eyes. "My love can't hold you here with me. My love has never had that kind of power and never will. Leave, Mack. The sooner the better."

"You sound so cold, so harsh," Mack said, shaking his head.

"I sound like a woman who is facing the truth." She lifted her chin. "Now, if you'll excuse me, I believe this conversation is over and I have a great deal of work to do."

"Go for it," Mack said, a rough edge to his voice as he got to his feet. "I have some telephone calls to make."

"Fine."

Mack strode from the room and Heather reached out one hand to grip the back of the computer chair, her other hand covering her mouth to stifle a sob that caught in her throat. She stumbled to the front of the chair and sank onto it, dropping her face into her hands.

Heather was unable to concentrate on her work during the next two hours, but she stayed in the bedroom. Mack did not return to rest on the bed. When she heard the sound of Melissa's and Emma's voices in the distance, she got to her feet, took a steadying breath and went into the living room, where she found not only the twins, but Susie and Buzzy, as well.

"Well, this is convenient," she said, hoping she sounded bright and cheerful but seriously doubting it. "Susie, Buzzy, I'm glad you're still here. You can say goodbye to Mack. Melissa, Emma, Uncle Mack is flying back to New York City. When is your flight, Mack?"

"Midnight," he said quietly from where he sat on the sofa.

"Ah, the Cinderella hour," Heather said, "when the fantasy is over and reality sets in."

"You're leaving?" Emma said, more in the form of a wail. "How come?"

"I, um, I need to see the specialist who is tending to my shoulder, Emma," Mack said. "It's important that I do that."

"But…" Melissa said, her bottom lip quivering. "I don't want you to go. Mommy, can't you tell Uncle Mack not to leave us?"

"No, sweetheart," Heather said, her heart aching, "I can't keep him here. We knew he'd be leaving…and…and now he is."

Susie narrowed her eyes, looked at Heather, then Mack, then back at Heather.

"There's something fishy going on here," Susie said.

"We had tuna fish sandwiches for lunch," Emma said. "Uncle Mack, don't you want to stay with us?"

"I…I can't, Emma," he said, his voice raspy. "Believe me, I would if I could, but…" He shook his head. "It's impossible. I, um, waited until you got back so I could say goodbye, but I'm going to the airport in a few minutes and I'll wait for my flight in the executive lounge. I can rest there and…it's better this way. You know, instead of us all sitting around being gloomy all evening."

"Fishier and fishier," Susie said, tapping one finger against her chin. "Heather, I need to see you out front for a minute. There's some weird-looking bugs on the leaves of your mulberry tree. Maybe they're planning on gobbling it up and it would be a shame to lose a lovely old tree like that one.''

''Can't it wait, Susie?'' Heather said.

''Heavens no,'' Susie said. ''We don't know how fast those little guys can eat. We'd better take a closer look at them, then decide if you need to call the landlord about having the tree sprayed or whatever. Come on.''

''Oh, for Pete's sake,'' Heather said, stomping across the room. ''This is all I need. Tree-eating bugs.''

As Heather and Susie left the house, Heather could hear the twins begging their uncle Mack not to leave for New York City. Heather sighed and marched to the tree, peering up at the leaves.

''I don't see any bugs, Susie,'' she said.

''There aren't any,'' Susie said. ''I wanted to get you alone. Talk to me, Heather. What's going on here? You and Mack both look like you just found out you're scheduled to have four root canals. You two are not happy campers. Why is he leaving in such a rush?''

Heather sniffled. ''Because…because he loves me.''

''Huh?''

''He does, Susie, he honest-to-goodness loves me and I love him and…but it's hopeless because Mack just can't be a tree, you know what I mean? He doesn't want roots, can't stay in one place, can't be a husband and father.''

"That's the craziest thing I've ever heard," Susie said, planting her hands on her hips.

"It's true," Heather said, blinking away her tears. "I've known that from conversations we had. I didn't mean to fall in love with him, because I knew he'd leave and now he is and...there's nothing I can do about it. Nothing can be changed. Not who Mack is, nor the fact that I was born under the wrong star or something and when I love, I lose, except for having the forever love of my daughters. There's no point in discussing this further, Susie. Facts are facts."

"People can change, Heather Marshall," Susie said none too quietly.

"Not this time." Heather turned and headed back toward the house.

"I don't believe this," Susie said, shaking her head as she followed Heather. "This is so sad, and...oh, I don't believe this."

Back in the living room Melissa was finishing buttoning Mack's shirt for him.

"There," she said, then kissed him on the cheek. "I'm really going to miss you, Uncle Mack."

"I'll miss you too, Melissa, and you, Emma. And Maxine and Buzzy and Susie and—"

"Our mom?" Emma said, hugging her kitten. "Are you going to miss our mommy?"

"Yes, Mack, do tell us," Susie said. "Are you going to miss Heather?"

Mack's head snapped up and he looked at Susie who was glaring at him.

"More than you know," he said, meeting her gaze directly.

"Oh, *I* know, but do *you?*" Susie said. "Don't you two realize what you're throwing away and—"

"Susie, please," Heather said. "Don't."

"I want to see the bugs on the tree," Buzzy said.

"It was a false alarm, sweetie," Susie said. "I thought there was something important happening around here, but I was wrong. It's obviously no big deal."

"Susie," Heather said, a warning tone to her voice, "that's enough."

"Fine. Okay. We're gone," Susie said, holding up her hands. "It was nice meeting you, Mack, and I hope your brain heals along with your shoulder. Goodbye. Buzzy say goodbye to Mack."

"'Bye, Mack," Buzzy said. "You're a cool guy."

"'Bye," Mack said quietly.

As Susie and Buzzy went out the front door, Mack announced that he was going to telephone for a taxi. Heather nodded and said she had work to do, and the twins plopped down on the floor in front of Mack, producing the saddest expressions they could muster, along with deep, dramatic sighs.

Twenty long minutes later, Heather shivered as she heard Emma yell that Uncle Mack's taxi had arrived.

No! Heather thought, getting to her feet. How was she going to find the strength to get through the next five minutes?

She walked slowly down the hall and into the living

room. The taxi driver was collecting Mack's suitcases and the twins were crying.

"Shh," Heather said, going to her daughters and wrapping her arms around them. "Don't you want Uncle Mack to remember you as smiling, happy girls?"

"No," Melissa said.

"I guess so," Emma said.

"Heather," Mack said, not looking directly at her, "I left a bunch of photographs for you on the kitchen table. I was planning on putting them in a really nice album first, but I didn't get the chance."

"Thank you," Heather said to the top of Melissa's head. "I'm sure we'll enjoy them."

"Ready, mister?" the taxi driver said.

No! Mack's mind hollered. He'd never be ready to leave this house, these kids, the only woman he'd ever loved. Hell, no!

"Yeah," he said. "Sure. Let's do it."

Mack closed the distance between Heather and the girls, tilted each twin's head up with one finger and kissed her on the forehead. Then he looked directly into Heather's tear-filled eyes.

"Goodbye, Heather," he said, his voice gritty. *Goodbye, my love.* "I'm...I'm sorry. I...thank you for everything."

Unable to speak past the sob in her throat, Heather nodded.

And then he was gone.

With a bang of the door and the rumble of a taxi that needed a new muffler, Mack Marshall was gone.

Emma burst into fresh tears and ran down the hall with Maxine in her arms. Melissa stomped her foot, sniffled a few times, then said she was going to play ball with Buzzy and wasn't going to think about Uncle Mack for even one second, so there.

Heather stood in the silent, empty room, and stared at the door. She simply stood there, miserable...and alone.

During the following hours Heather felt like a robot performing her duties without thinking. She joined the twins in gushing over the wonderful photographs Mack had given them, finished an income tax return, prepared dinner, cleaned the kitchen, then listened to the girls' prayers at bedtime. Prayers that included the request to please bless Uncle Mack.

The twins went to sleep quickly, being physically and emotionally exhausted, and Heather wandered around the small living room, feeling restless, edgy and so unhappy she was sure she could cry for a week without stopping.

She sank onto the sofa, leaned her head on the top and stared at the ceiling.

"To love is to lose," she whispered. "I know that. That doesn't include Melissa and Emma, of course, because..."

Heather stopped speaking and sat up straight, her mind racing.

Because she had been determined to keep her babies, no matter what, she thought suddenly. She loved them with her whole heart and nothing, or no one, would ever separate her from them. She'd known that from the moment she'd seen them being born. They were hers and she was theirs...forever.

There had been a well-intentioned social worker who had visited her in the hospital when the girls were born, a woman who gently suggested that the best thing for Heather's babies might be to give them up for adoption. Heather was a young woman alone with no money or marketable skills that would produce the income she would need to raise her babies.

No, no, no, she had told the woman. She intended to keep her daughters, make whatever sacrifices were necessary to have them with her. They were hers, a part of who she was, and they belonged with her. Oh, yes, her babies were worth fighting for, no matter what.

Heather got slowly to her feet, her heart racing. "And...and so is Mack Marshall."

So what was she going to do about it?

Mack sat on a plush sofa in the executive lounge at the airport, rotating his injured shoulder as he held the telephone receiver in his other hand.

"No, Marilyn, I'm not interested in contracting to go to Ireland after my shoulder gets its act together."

"It's big bucks, Mack," Marilyn said. "As your agent..." She laughed. "I want my cut of that money pie."

"Nope. Sorry."

"Well, how about an assignment in Alaska?" Marilyn asked. "The offer isn't as good, but I think I can jack them up a bit to meet our price. Or throw a dart at a world map and just go. I can sell whatever you produce. So? Where? Africa? China? Spain?"

"No," Mack said.

"Well, cripe, Mack, what do you want to do when you're back on your feet?"

"My feet," he said, "would like to stay in one place for a stretch of time. I'm going to do another book. I just decided that in the last few hours as I've been sitting here. I'm going to call it 'Faces of War…Faces of Peace.'" Images of the photographs he'd taken of Heather, the twins and the people on their block flashed before Mack's eyes. "I've got some great stuff already."

"Fantastic," Marilyn said. "I've got an editor waiting with baited breath and a blank check. Top-of-the-line cruise, here I come." She paused. "I thought for sure you were a goner in the heart department out there, but you're coming back to New York and settling in for a spell here, huh?"

"Yes, staying put is what feels right," Mack said, nodding. "I've had enough of living out of a suitcase and…and…not having any sense of really belonging anywhere…not having any roots. I want to buy a house too, with a yard, grass and…" Mack's eyes widened and his heart beat so wildly he could hear the echo of it in his ears. "Oh…my…God."

"What? What?" Marilyn said. "Is someone hijacking the airport? What's wrong? Mack? Are you there?''

''I've been so busy making it clear who I've always been,'' he said, an incredulous tone to his voice, ''that I didn't pay enough attention to who I've become. I'm a tree, Marilyn. *I'm a tree!*''

''Is that one of those trick answers?'' Marilyn said. ''Please tell me I'm not supposed to understand what you're talking about, because I don't have a clue.''

''I've got to go.''

''I thought your flight didn't leave until midnight,'' Marilyn said.

''It doesn't,'' Mack said, ''but if I'm not too late, I won't be on it.''

''Now *that,*'' Marilyn said, ''*really* didn't make sense, Mack Marshall. Not too late for what?''

''My dream,'' Mack said. ''Wish me luck. 'Bye.''

''Right. Get lots of rest on the flight home. You definitely need it. See you soon, Mack.''

Mack dropped the receiver back into place and got to his feet, gripping his left arm as he rose. He strode across the large, lushly furnished room that he'd had all to himself since arriving at the airport hours before.

As he extended his right arm to push open the door, someone pulled it from the other side, causing Mack to snap his hand to the side just before smacking the head of the person attempting to enter.

''Heather,'' Mack said, staring at her. ''Heather? What are you doing here? I was just leaving to...''

''Excuse me, ma'am,'' a man said, coming up behind Heather, "but I need to see your membership card before you can enter the executive suite."

"Oh," Heather said. "Oh, dear, I don't..."

"It's fine," Mack said, taking Heather's hand and pulling her forward. "She's with me. No problem."

The man nodded and closed the door, leaving the pair alone in the large room with Mack still holding Heather's hand.

"You're here," Mack said, frowning slightly. "Heather, why are you here?"

"May I sit down, please?" Heather said, afraid her trembling legs would refuse to support her much longer.

"Oh, yeah, sure. Do you want something to drink? Eat? They have all kinds of stuff in here and... Can I get you a soda, sandwich, potato chips or...why are you here?" Mack paused. "Wait a minute. It's past the twins' bedtime. What did you do with them?"

"Becky is with the girls." Heather crossed the room and sat in an easy chair. "I called and told her I had an emergency meeting with one of my accounting clients and she agreed to spend the night on the sofa if I got back later than when she'd go to bed on a school night."

Mack pulled another easy chair in front of Heather's and sat, their knees almost touching.

"You said...you said you were just leaving," Heather said. "Am I keeping you from something?"

"No, no, forget that," Mack said. "I'm starting to sound like a broken record, but why are you here?"

Heather clutched her hands tightly in her lap, lifted her chin and looked directly into Mack's dark eyes.

"Mack," she said, wishing her voice was steadier, "I love you. When I realized the depths of my feelings for you, I was devastated because I believed that to love is to lose, to cry, to be lonely, instead of just alone. That's the way love has always been for me and, sure enough, there you were, saying you were leaving, just as I knew you would."

"But..."

"Please, hear me out."

Mack nodded.

"But then," Heather went on, "I remembered how fiercely determined I was to keep my babies when they were born, to fight for them, to make whatever sacrifices were necessary to keep them with me. And they *are* with me, and we share forever love. I broke the heartbreaking cycle of loving and losing when I gathered my daughters close and held on tightly to them.

"But with you? Realizing I was in love with you? I slipped back to before the twins were born, accepted without question that loving you was a mistake, that I had guaranteed myself a future of crying alone in the night."

"Ah, Heather, I..."

"Hush."

"'Kay," Mack said.

"Mack," Heather said, her eyes filling with tears, "love, true love, between a man and a woman requires give-and-take, compromise, sacrifices if necessary, whatever is needed if those two people are determined to be together.

"I came here to state my case, to fight for you, if you want to put it that way. I love you so much and I'm willing to accept that you need to have space, need to travel and be on the move. If you can cut back on those trips, be with me, with your family, for at least half of the time, I truly believe we can make this work. We can, Mack." A sob caught in Heather's throat. "If you want it—me…the twins—badly enough. If you truly, truly love me."

"Oh, Heather." Mack closed his eyes for a moment in an attempt to gain control of his raging emotions, but was unable to keep tears from shimmering in his eyes. "Yes. Yes, I love you with my whole heart, with all that I am. And I love the girls and the babies we'll have later and—

"When you came in, I said I was leaving. I was on my way back to you, to tell you that as I sat here alone in this room for all these hours I realized that I *had* changed without even knowing it. I'd accepted for years what my father said, that I had inherited his wanderlust spirit and nothing could be done about it. But he was wrong, and I was wrong to accept it for so long.

"Well, not anymore. Not…anymore." Mack cleared his throat, but his voice remained choked with emotion. "I'm going to stay put and write a book, Heather, because I don't want to travel the world, dodge bullets, be the hot-shot photojournalist I've been for so very long. When I do travel, it will be in the summer when I can take my family with me to nice places, like England, Scotland and...I can open a photography studio, or maybe teach photography, or—

"All I know is, I love you, I want to spend the rest of my life with you and...Heather, please believe me. I'm...I'm a tree. At long last, I'm an honest-to-goodness tree."

"Oh, Mack," Heather said, tears spilling onto her cheeks.

"Heather Marshall," Mack said, "will you marry me, be my wife, my partner in life, until death parts us?"

"Yes," she whispered. "Oh, yes."

Mack reached out a shaking hand and Heather placed her hand in his. He pulled her forward to sit on his right thigh, then cupped the back of her head as he raised his lips to meet hers.

The kiss tasted like salty tears. The kiss was a commitment to the forever they would share, the future that was spread in front of them with the lush bounty of what was yet to come. The kiss ignited desire within them that they welcomed. The kiss was theirs and they rejoiced in the wonder of it.

Heather slowly and reluctantly lifted her head and smiled at Mack through tears of joy.

"Mack," she said, "let's go home."

Epilogue

The large ranch-style house sat on an acre of land on a rise that afforded a marvelous view of the mountains surrounding Tucson and the glittering city lights below.

The house was so newly constructed that no landscaping had yet been done, nor had pictures been hung on the walls within. Some of the rooms were still unfurnished, but a block wall had been finished around the backyard so that a dog named Butch, who was a funny-looking, much-loved mixed breed, couldn't wander away to explore the desert. Butch was curled up asleep on the patio with Maxine, the cat, tucked beneath his chin.

Inside the house a warm and welcoming fire crackled in the flagstone fireplace in the large living room. A tall Christmas tree stood by the floor-to-ceiling windows that made up the entire front wall of the room.

Mack sat on the floor in front of the hearth, his back resting against the sofa behind him as he stared into the leaping flames.

"A penny for your thoughts," Heather said, sitting next to him and nestling close to his side.

He kissed her on the forehead. "I was just thinking that we actually did it. We were determined to be in this house by Christmas and here we are, still living out of boxes to a point, but we're here, by gum."

Heather laughed. "You bet. Our daughters are snug as bugs in their sleeping bags in their separate bedrooms because their new beds haven't been delivered yet, but they are happy little girls."

"And you, Mrs. Marshall?" Mack said. "Are you happy?"

"Oh, Mack, if I get any happier, I'll probably pop a seam. And you?"

"Hey, I'm a man who has achieved his dream. It doesn't get any better than this."

Heather glanced around the room. "A new house. This was my dream, the twins' dream for so long." She inhaled deeply. "I can still smell the lingering aroma of paint. Isn't that super?"

Mack chuckled. "If you say so."

"What I say is that I love you, Mack Marshall, more than I can ever begin to put into words."

"Sometimes," he said, lowering his head to hers, "words just aren't necessary."

Their lips met and heated desire flared within them instantly, hotter than the flames in the hearth. They broke the kiss only long enough to shed clothing before kissing, caressing, touching every inch of each other. Passions soared to heights that continually amazed them, the want and need never fully quelled.

They stretched out on the plush carpeting, the flames of the fire casting golden hues over their naked bodies that glistened in the firelight.

They teased and tantalized until they could bear no more.

"I want you, Mack," Heather whispered. "I love you and want you so very much."

He entered her, joining their bodies just as their hearts had been joined months before. They moved as one, synchronized to perfection, the heat coiling tighter within them as they came closer and closer to the place they could only go together.

"Mack!"

"I love you, Heather," he said. "Forever."

They were flung into glorious oblivion, clinging to each other, then floated slowly back. Mack moved off of Heather and tucked her close to his side as they savored the sated pleasure consuming them.

"Merry Christmas, Mack," Heather said sleepily.

"Merry Christmas, my love," Mack said, then wrapped his arm around her waist as though he'd never again let her go.

"And many, many more."

Mr. and Mrs. Mack Marshall, daughters Melissa and Emma, pets Butch and Maxine...were home.

* * * * *

*Don't miss Joan Elliott Pickart's
exciting new single title,*

Party of Three,

*coming only to Silhouette Books
in August 2001.*

*And now for a sneak preview,
please turn the page.*

Chapter One

" Are you in charge of this place?"

Jessica blinked. "Pardon me?"

"Is that a tough question, lady?" the man said. "Are you, or are you not, running this shelter? Because if you are, you're doing a lousy job of it."

Three realizations tumbled one into the next in Jessica MacAllister's beleaguered brain.

One...this rude individual was a member of the Ventura Police Department, her mind catalogued.

Two...this rude individual was, without a doubt, one of the most ruggedly handsome men she'd ever seen in her just-celebrated-her-thirtieth-birthday life. He had wavy black hair that was wet from the rain, dark eyes and tawny skin, shoulders as wide as a city block, and masculine features that appeared as though they'd been chiseled roughly from stone.

And three...this rude individual had swished her depleted, nervous wreck state into oblivion and replaced it with rip-roaring, made-as-hell anger.

Jessica planted her hands flat on the top of the desk and rose to her feet slowly, her narrow-eyed gaze focused on the rude individual. She straightened and folded her arms beneath her breasts.

"Just who do you think you are," she said. "Mr. Whatever Your Name Is, coming in here telling me this shelter isn't managed well? You've got a lot of nerve, do you know that? Or is that too tough a question for you? I want you to leave. Now."

Beautiful when angry, Daniel thought, his gaze riveted on the irate woman before him. He was witnessing a whole new meaning to that old cliché. She was sensational. Her big, dark brown eyes were flashing like laser beams, her cheeks were flushed a pretty pink and her kissable lips were tightly together, just waiting to be teased apart.

"Hello?" Jessica said. "No, cancel that. The word I want is goodbye. You're leaving."

Daniel thudded back to reality from the rather hazy, sensual place he'd just floated off to and matched the woman's pose of crossing his arms over his chest.

"I'm Lieutenant Daniel Quinn," he said. "Homicide. Ventura Police Department. And you are?"

"Insulted to the maximum," Jessica said, lifting her chin. "I'm also Jessica MacAllister, Attorney-at-Law, since you feel it's important to fling titles around. Homicide? What are you doing here? No one was hurt, let alone killed, for mercy's sake.''

''No one was killed this time,'' Daniel said, nearly shouting. ''But what about the next episode like this and the one after that? Why in the hell isn't there an armed security guard on duty at this place twenty-four hours a day, Mrs....Miss...?''

''It's Ms., Lieutenant,'' Jessica said tightly, ''and we have no security guard because there aren't funds to pay one.''

''Then you should close this place down until you have the money to hire him,'' Daniel bellowed. ''Without an armed guard this isn't a shelter. It's a tragedy waiting to happen.''

''Oh-h-h, you are so off base, it's a crime,'' Jessica said, nearly sputtering. ''You should arrest yourself, Lieutenant.
There...is...no...money...for...an...armed guard. Is it clear yet?''

''You're wrong, Ms...Jessica,'' he said, his voice suddenly quiet and weary sounding. He looked directly into her big, brown eyes as he spoke. ''What happened here tonight should have proved that to you. If that guy would have gotten inside this building before the uniforms arrived, someone, maybe a lot of someones, would be dead now. Dead is...dead is forever, Jessica. No second chances. No way to undo it, change things, turn back the clock and handle it differently. You've got to listen to what I'm saying to you.''

''I...I am but...'' Jessica started, then stopped. She turned and snatched up the heavy envelope from the top of her desk. ''See this? It's the papers needed to apply for a grant, which I intend to do to hopefully obtain funds for The Peaceful Dove.

''Since you're so determined that there should be an armed guard on staff at all times, then you can help me fill out these forms and make your pitch for the money to pay that person. How does hours and hours of tedious paperwork sound, Lieutenant? I think you're about to sing a different tune.''

''Wrong,'' Daniel said. ''I'll be in touch with you very soon and we'll make arrangements to get together and start working on that application.''

Jessica's smile slid off her chin and her eyes widened. ''What?''

''Good night, Ms...Jessica,'' Daniel said, smiling. ''I think since we're going to be spending...to quote...hours and hours together doing some tedious paperwork we ought to be on first-name basis, don't you? You bet.''

* * * * *

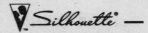

Feel like a star with Silhouette.

We will fly you and a guest to New York City for an exciting weekend stay at a glamorous 5-star hotel. Experience a refreshing day at one of New York's trendiest spas and have your photo taken by a professional. Plus, receive $1,000 U.S. spending money!

Flowers...long walks...dinner for two... how does Silhouette Books make romance come alive for you?

Send us a script, with 500 words or less, along with visuals (only drawings, magazine cutouts or photographs or combination thereof). Show us how Silhouette Makes Your Love Come Alive. Be creative and have fun. No purchase necessary. All entries must be clearly marked with your name, address and telephone number. All entries will become property of Silhouette and are not returnable. **Contest closes September 28, 2001.**

Please send your entry to: **Silhouette Makes You a Star!**

In U.S.A.
P.O. Box 9069
Buffalo, NY, 14269-9069

In Canada
P.O. Box 637
Fort Erie, ON, L2A 5X3

Look for contest details on the next page, by visiting www.eHarlequin.com or request a copy by sending a self-addressed envelope to the applicable address above. Contest open to Canadian and U.S. residents who are 18 or over. Void where prohibited.

Where love comes alive™

Our lucky winner's photo will appear in a Silhouette ad. Join the fun!

SRMYAS1

HARLEQUIN "SILHOUETTE MAKES YOU A STAR!" CONTEST 1308
OFFICIAL RULES
NO PURCHASE NECESSARY TO ENTER

1. To enter, follow directions published in the offer to which you are responding. Contest begins June 1, 2001, and ends on September 28, 2001. Entries must be postmarked by September 28, 2001, and received by October 5, 2001. Enter by hand-printing (or typing) on an 8 ½" x 11" piece of paper your name, address (including zip code), contest number/name and attaching a script containing 500 words or less, along with drawings, photographs or magazine cutouts, or combinations thereof (i.e., collage) on no larger than 9" x 12" piece of paper, describing how the Silhouette books make romance come alive for you. Mail via first-class mail to: Harlequin "Silhouette Makes You a Star!" Contest 1308, (in the U.S.) P.O. Box 9069, Buffalo, NY 14269-9069, (in Canada) P.O. Box 637, Fort Erie, Ontario, Canada L2A 5X3. Limit one entry per person, household or organization.

2. Contests will be judged by a panel of members of the Harlequin editorial, marketing and public relations staff. Fifty percent of criteria will be judged against script and fifty percent will be judged against drawing, photographs and/or magazine cutouts. Judging criteria will be based on the following:

   - Sincerity—25%
   - Originality and Creativity—50%
   - Emotionally Compelling—25%

   In the event of a tie, duplicate prizes will be awarded. Decisions of the judges are final.

3. All entries become the property of Torstar Corp. and may be used for future promotional purposes. Entries will not be returned. No responsibility is assumed for lost, late, illegible, incomplete, inaccurate, nondelivered or misdirected mail.

4. Contest open only to residents of the U.S. (except Puerto Rico) and Canada who are 18 years of age or older, and is void wherever prohibited by law; all applicable laws and regulations apply. Any litigation within the Province of Quebec respecting the conduct or organization of a publicity contest may be submitted to the Régie des alcools, des courses et des jeux for a ruling. Any litigation respecting the awarding of a prize may be submitted to the Régie des alcools, des courses et des jeux only for the purpose of helping the parties reach a settlement. Employees and immediate family members of Torstar Corp. and D. L. Blair, Inc., their affiliates, subsidiaries and all other agencies, entities and persons connected with the use, marketing or conduct of this contest are not eligible to enter. Taxes on prizes are the sole responsibility of the winner. Acceptance of any prize offered constitutes permission to use winner's name, photograph or other likeness for the purposes of advertising, trade and promotion on behalf of Torstar Corp., its affiliates and subsidiaries without further compensation to the winner, unless prohibited by law.

5. Winner will be determined no later than November 30, 2001, and will be notified by mail. Winner will be required to sign and return an Affidavit of Eligibility/Release of Liability/Publicity Release form within 15 days after winner notification. Noncompliance within that time period may result in disqualification and an alternative winner may be selected. All travelers must execute a Release of Liability prior to ticketing and must possess required travel documents (e.g., passport, photo ID) where applicable. Trip must be booked by December 31, 2001, and completed within one year of notification. No substitution of prize permitted by winner. Torstar Corp. and D. L. Blair, Inc., their parents, affiliates and subsidiaries are not responsible for errors in printing of contest, entries and/or game pieces. In the event of printing or other errors that may result in unintended prize values or duplication of prizes, all affected game pieces or entries shall be null and void. **Purchase or acceptance of a product offer does not improve your chances of winning.**

6. Prizes: (1) Grand Prize—A 2-night/3-day trip for two (2) to New York City, including round-trip coach air transportation nearest winner's home and hotel accommodations (double occupancy) at The Plaza Hotel, a glamorous afternoon makeover at a trendy New York spa, $1,000 in U.S. spending money and an opportunity to have a professional photo taken and appear in a Silhouette advertisement (approximate retail value: $7,000). (10) Ten Runner-Up Prizes of gift packages (retail value $50 ea.). Prizes consist of only those items listed as part of the prize. Limit one prize per person. Prize is valued in U.S. currency.

7. For the name of the winner (available after December 31, 2001) send a self-addressed, stamped envelope to: Harlequin "Silhouette Makes You a Star!" Contest 1197 Winners, P.O. Box 4200 Blair, NE 68009-4200 or you may access the www.eHarlequin.com Web site through February 28, 2002.

Contest sponsored by Torstar Corp., P.O Box 9042, Buffalo, NY 14269-9042.

SRMYAS2

If you enjoyed what you just read,
then we've got an offer you can't resist!

Take 2 bestselling love stories FREE!

Plus get a FREE surprise gift!

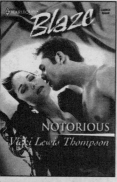